HUNTING MONSTERS

AN EDGE OF HUMANITY NOVEL

STEFON MEARS

Also by Stefon Mears

Cavan Oltblood Series
Half a Wizard
The Ice Dagger
Spells of Undeath

Spells for Hire
Devil's Shoestring
Zombie Powder
Spirit Trap
Dragon's Blood (coming December 2019)

The Rise of Magic
Magician's Choice
Sleight of Mind
Lunar Alchemy
Three Fae Monte
The Sphinx Principle

The Telepath Trilogy
Surviving Telepathy
Immoral Telepathy
Targeting Telepathy

Edge of Humanity
Caught Between Monsters
Hunting Monsters

Power City Tales
Not Quite Bulletproof
No Money in Heroism

Devil's Night
Portal-Land, Oregon
Stealing from Pirates
Fade to Gold
With a Broken Sword
Twice Against the Dragon
The House on Cedar Street
Sudden Death
On the Edge of Faerie
Confronting Legends (Spells & Swords Vol. 1)
Uncle Stone Teeth and Other Macabre Poems
The Patreon Collection, Vol. 1-4 (Vol. 5, coming soon)

Published by Thousand Faces Publishing, Portland, Oregon

http://1kfaces.com

ISBN: 978-1-948490-15-3

Also by Stefon Mears

Cavan Oltblood Series
Half a Wizard
The Ice Dagger
Spells of Undeath

Spells for Hire
Devil's Shoestring
Zombie Powder
Spirit Trap
Dragon's Blood (coming December 2019)

The Rise of Magic
Magician's Choice
Sleight of Mind
Lunar Alchemy
Three Fae Monte
The Sphinx Principle

The Telepath Trilogy
Surviving Telepathy
Immoral Telepathy
Targeting Telepathy

Edge of Humanity
Caught Between Monsters
Hunting Monsters

Power City Tales
Not Quite Bulletproof
No Money in Heroism

Devil's Night
Portal-Land, Oregon
Stealing from Pirates
Fade to Gold
With a Broken Sword
Twice Against the Dragon
The House on Cedar Street
Sudden Death
On the Edge of Faerie
Confronting Legends (Spells & Swords Vol. 1)
Uncle Stone Teeth and Other Macabre Poems
The Patreon Collection, Vol. 1-4 (Vol. 5, coming soon)

Published by Thousand Faces Publishing, Portland, Oregon

http://1kfaces.com

Copyright © 2018 by Stefon Mears

Front cover image of the man in shadow © Pryzmat | Dreamstime.com

ISBN: 978-1-948490-15-3

Hunting Monsters

An *Edge of Humanity* novel

1

IT WAS JUST SUPPOSED TO BE A GHOST HUNT. BUSINESS AS USUAL.

But nothing about that night was usual. Even before it all went to hell.

It was somewhere around nine o'clock when I ground the van to a halt, kicking up little dust and gravel, but more than I expected. Driven through two flash storms, out here in the boondocks of Missouri, and I figured the whole countryside would be sopping wet by the time we finally reached this damned little crossroads.

Guess those storms were more localized than I thought.

Wish the heat was. It was an August night, and apparently in Missouri that meant hot and muggy. Van's air conditioner had worked overtime to keep us comfortable, but it was time to abandon comfort and do what we'd come here to do.

"We're here. Everybody out," I said. "I'll be along in a second."

Todd was the first one out, of course. Good for him. Getting out of my face right now was the smartest thing he ever did, and this was a guy with two advanced college degrees. Doctorates. Parapsychology and Psychology. Got 'em both at the same time, even.

Totally unfair, that. To be smart as Todd, as educated, and still have the all-American good looks and camera presence that he could have lit Hollywood on fire if he'd ever decided to do more than our little television show.

But he was like Page. True believers, out to bring proof to the world. That's why our show was called *Seekers*. As in, seeking the truth about the paranormal.

Mostly, that meant ghost hunting. Like tonight.

You'd think a guy with so many checks in the plus column would be patient by nature. Maybe calm and collected enough to not spend three hours yelling at the driver for having trouble following a set of scant, handwritten directions, in a part of the country I'd never been to before.

Hell, it wasn't even me Todd was really mad at. Part of the reason I hadn't called him on it.

Yet.

But that was Todd.

Page followed him right out, no doubt as tired of listening to his bitching as Tangi and I were. She never called Todd on his temper though. Didn't want his fits to interfere with the work.

Page, she was our other on-air talent. Had a Parapsychology doctorate too, but never bothered with any other. Though between the two of them, she was the one with all the patents.

And she even beat Todd on looks. That smooth, dark coffee skin, and swimsuit model build. All to go with a southern belle accent that could make me smile, even while Todd was yelling at me.

Todd and Page's looks were the main reason anyone tuned into our little off-brand cable network show. If we could have gotten them to loosen up on their wardrobe — ditch the suits and show a little more skin — our ratings would have gone through the roof.

Page closed the van door behind her with a soft thump that was as close as she came to slamming any door.

For a moment I could focus on the ticking of the van's engine.

It didn't help. I was too wound up from three hours of getting yelled at through Missouri backroads in a van without all-wheel drive.

Once Page was outside, it was just me and Tangi in the van. We were the behind-the-scenes talent that kept our show clicking. He sat in the passenger seat next to me, as usual.

Tangi was a huge Samoan guy, and this is *me* calling him huge. I used to play linebacker for U.C.L.A. when I was in film school. But Tangi made me feel downright small. Most of it was muscle too, like me.

Tangi, though, had the kind of deep bass voice that even made Todd's panty-dropping baritone envious.

"You counted to ten yet?" Tangi asked, with the nigh-infinite patience he attributed to regular meditation.

"More like a hundred," I growled. My shoulders and arms were still so tight, I wasn't sure I could pry my fingers off the steering wheel without them immediately leaping for Todd's throat.

Yeah, I'd known all three of my partners since college and yeah, I'd long since gotten used to Todd's yelling fits.

But even I had limits.

"Just breathe, baby," Tangi said. "Just breathe. And save it for the game."

Save it for the game. An old joke, and one I didn't think Tangi knew about. Must have been saving it for a special occasion.

Any time I had a temper flare up in college, coach told me to save it for the game. The rest of the team picked up on it.

I heard that phrase a lot in college. But only around my teammates.

To hear those words come out of *Tangi*, eight years out of U.C.L.A., was unexpected enough that I snorted a laugh.

Then Tangi started his infectious chuckle, and soon I was leaning my forehead on the steering wheel, laughing despite myself.

"Can we get this started tonight?" Todd called from somewhere out of eyeshot.

I stopped laughing. Started again on the deep breaths through my nose.

"Safe for you to come out?" Tangi asked, side-eyeing me.

He held up an offering. The Twinkie of Peace.

"Depends," I said, looking from the Twinkie to Tangi and back. "If

Todd says one more wrong word to me before he apologizes, I'm going to go Joshua Tree on his ass."

Joshua Tree state park. The last time Todd had yelled at me for that long. I'd let him yell himself out, and everyone thought things were cool.

He then said one more wrong thing and I dropped him like a quarterback who hadn't even known the blitz was coming.

Lucky for Todd that Tangi was there to separate us before things got out of hand. Kept the pretty boy's nose unbroken.

Right now, in the van, Tangi played peacemaker again. Waved the Twinkie at me.

"That from you or Todd?" I asked, narrowing my eyes.

"It's from Page. She doesn't want to be here all night, and she doesn't want to have to do reshoots if you give Todd a bloody nose or a busted lip."

"Fine," I said, mollified that Page was that thoughtful.

Page and I had never ever tried to date. I'd never asked her. At first, because she had a boyfriend when the four of us met, junior year.

Then, well, I just never figured Page could be interested in me, so I never bothered asking.

Despite what some guys will tell you, being friends with a beautiful girl — just friends, I mean — can be just like being friends with anyone else. Even if you find you still enjoy that sight and sound of her.

I mean, we were friends. I wasn't suddenly blind and deaf.

So I accepted the Twinkie, and downed it in the traditional one bite.

Tangi nodded. Clapped me on the back, then went to get his cameras and lights.

I swallowed the treat down, the unsnapped my seat belt and hopped out of the van.

MIGHT AS WELL HAVE BEEN A STEAM BATH OUT HERE. THE MOMENT I was out of the van, wet heat just enveloped me. Glued my tan polo shirt and slacks to me in nothing flat.

How the dirt beneath my Puma's wasn't mud didn't click with me. I mean, yeah, it wasn't exactly dusty, but it wasn't all that soft either. Must have been baked solid during the day or something.

I forced myself not to look at Todd. Not yet.

I looked up at the vast sea of stars overhead. Way more than I was used to back in California, and one of the few nice things about being this far outside anything like a city.

Amazing. Great distraction, too. Gave me something to focus on for a few breaths and ease some of the tension out of my muscles. And a chance to ignore the hushed voice of Page, quietly talking to Todd somewhere nearby.

A little stretching helped too.

Then I saw the side of the van without the distraction of loading it with gear.

Our *Seekers* logo — a stylized S, holding a magnifying glass — had been hastily applied to the side of the white van via vinyl signage. Clearly done at the last minute. Probably because some network jerk decided not to give us our usual rough-and-tumble SUV as part of the whole pissing contest.

Didn't do great things for my mood.

I wanted to blame Todd for the pissing contest, but honestly it was as much Page as Todd making it happen.

Didn't make me any happier that they got us sent out into the boondocks of Missouri, chasing a ghost that no one even wrote about on the internet.

I mean honestly. How big a haunting could it be, if no one local was bragging about it online?

Just one more thing to grumble about as I slammed the van door shut behind me.

I had to admit, though, the place had a good look for a haunted crossroads. Two narrow strips of rocky, uneven dirt, intersecting near a wooden sign so old I had no prayer of reading what places it was pointing to.

If those places even existed anymore.

I had no doubt Tangi could get some great, atmospheric shots to go with the few we'd picked up earlier of the flash storms.

Rain and lightning always set a great mood for our show, even if they made shooting hell.

The air here at the crossroads smelled thick with the kind of vegetation I never saw growing up in the wild suburbs of the San Francisco Bay Area. Couldn't even begin to pick it apart.

Some of the trees looked like oaks. Couldn't identify the others, or even hazard a guess what any of the plants were.

Well, apart from the thick wild grass, I mean.

Maybe that was what I was smelling. Whatever it was, it hit Tangi's allergies all wrong, and the big man started sneezing even before he had his rig set up.

And when a guy as big as Tangi sneezes, you can't miss it. Like the fifteen-inch gun on a battleship going off.

We all blessed him with one voice, then I turned and started my usual checks, beginning with the batteries, continuing on into the disc space for our audio, then separating the mics.

I wasn't thrilled with our chances of getting great sound out here. No real breeze, which was something — wind could play *hell* on mics — but with all the crickets, frogs, cicadas and such, it was louder than a New York street out here.

That was a problem for later. If we needed to find a studio for a bunch of dub work, it would serve the network right.

As I was getting the sound equipment organized, I could hear footsteps crunching closer.

Weren't heavy enough to be Tangi, and no way Page was going to approach until Todd and I hashed things out.

Had to be Todd then.

I didn't look up. Just kept on with setup.

Todd cleared his throat.

I ignored him.

"Come on, Sel," Todd said, cajoling, like I was one of his conquests. "It wasn't you I was mad at."

Battery packs all looked good. Mics were fine. Mixer was handling power and phantom power just fine. Be better if I could handle the boom for this, but we'd have to work with a rig. Page already said she wanted me on white noise detail.

"Look at me, Sel," Todd said. "Please?"

That was a word worth turning around for.

Todd stood there, suffering more in his neat black silk suit, than I was in my cotton. That pleased me. His hundred-dollar haircut was already bent out of shape by the humidity.

I should have spoken next. After all, I'd accepted the Twinkie of Peace. But I was still on edge, and we both knew it.

"I'm sorry, Sel," Todd said, and I could see it even more in his blue eyes than I could hear in his voice. "It wasn't you. These damned dirt roads, maybe, but not you. You did the best you could, and I know it."

I was with him up until the "best you could" crack.

I could feel the frown take shape.

Todd's hands came up.

"Sorry!" he said again. "Really, Sel. I'm sorry. It's just..." He shook his head. "We shouldn't be here. We should be in a studio with Mr. Xerxes, either confirming his amazing claims or debunking him."

Mr. Xerxes. The source of the pissing contest. Guy was a psychic, claimed he could do remote viewing. Claimed he could read Zener cards right ninety-eight times out of a hundred, no matter who was looking at them. Even if they were in a sealed envelope until after he read them.

Didn't even have to be in the same building, from what he claimed.

Todd and Page had been all hot and bothered to get Mr. Xerxes into the studio. Went to the mat with the brass over it.

The brass said psychics were lousy television. Claimed our viewers wanted us out in the field. Bringing them Americana and hunting ghosts.

I thought the viewers just wanted to gawk at Todd and Page, but some of them probably wanted to see the sights and hear the histories.

But Todd was still talking.

"I'm sorry I took it out on you," Todd said. "You don't deserve that."

I nodded. "Thanks, Todd."

Todd flashed me the smile they put on half our posters.

"Now go get set up, I need to record some atmosphere before we get started."

I did, too, but mostly I wanted him out of my face. I'd forgive him, all right. I always did. But right then, I needed time to cool off.

And in this heat, that was no easy feat.

Maybe twenty minutes later, Tangi had the lights and cameras set up. I had the sound squared away, and we were ready to roll.

Anytime now, the ghost of some old blues musician was supposed to show up at this tiny little excuse for a crossroads, and play his guitar. Word we'd gotten was that he did this every night, waiting for the devil to come give him back his soul.

And if he showed up, we'd be here to record it.

* * *

"Fuck!"

That was Page's assessment of the situation, after about three hours of waiting.

It was just after midnight. Not much cooler yet, and still just as noisy with the wildlife.

No strains of blues guitar, though, and I'd checked all the mics and everything we'd picked up. Even the white noise mic. Did it every half-hour or so, just in case there was something we couldn't hear with the naked ear.

Nothing so far.

Tangi wasn't having any better with the cameras. Not even the ones Page had designed, based off the old Kirlian photography approach.

Another night when the ghosts were failing to show.

Frankly, they'd never shown up yet. Not in my opinion, anyway. Page and Todd, though, they interpreted some of our "findings" differently. Every week they found elements or moments to gush at our viewers over.

This week, I'd already been figuring they'd have to stretch pretty hard for anything they could call "evidence."

Still, I never expected Page to erupt like that.

Yeah, I know. It was only one word. But for *Page*, that was an explosion. Page swore the way most people paid taxes — infrequently, and only under duress.

That one word from Page had me wide awake and hustling to where she stood in the middle of the crossroads. Me and everybody else.

Todd had been wandering up and down the dirt roads a bit, hoping to find some sign on the ghost-seeker that Page designed. Looked kind of like a handheld oscilloscope, with waves in green, red and amber.

Something to do with reading tiny electromagnetic fluctuations.

He'd had no better results than the rest of us, or he'd've said something.

But the moment Page let fly a curse word, all three of the rest of us snapped to her.

"This is a snipe hunt," Page said, and she started pacing. "The brass probably made the whole thing up. Punishment for fighting them about Mr. Xerxes."

"We should give it more time," Todd said, voice careful. He knew he'd already pissed one of us off tonight. "It's only just midnight. If we—"

"No," Page said, and her tone brooked no debate. Page could get this determined look in her eye. Gave her a kind of laser focus that had nothing to do with look, and everything to do with...

Charisma. That was the only word I had for it. But when Page had that look in her eye, none of us wanted to go against her.

And I have to admit, we put that look on camera as often as we could. Especially for a commercial cut. No way anyone was turning away from the sight of a determined Page.

"What then?" Tangi said, his deep voice lacking anything like challenge. I never knew how he did that.

"I have a better solution." Page smiled.

"The brass said we had to come back from this with a show," Todd said, and he was trying to sound as neutral as Tangi, but he couldn't pull it off either.

"And we will," Page said.

She had all our attention. She knew it. She still made us wait a moment. Leaned in a little. Spoke softly, as though someone might overhear, even though I doubted there was another soul — living or dead — for miles.

"Remember when we were buying gas?"

"Sure," I said without thinking. "It was the only break I got from Todd's yelling."

That got a snicker out of Tangi, but it died under the intensity of Page's eyes.

Hadn't been much of a gas station. Single pump, with not much more than a shed to keep the rain off the attendant, and provide a theoretically lockable place for the snacks and drinks they sold.

"I spent some time talking to the cashier," she said.

Todd nodded. Standard procedure for us, whenever we were nearing a site. If the local was male, Page spoke to him. If female, Todd handled it.

Flirt a little, praise a little, listen a lot. People loved to talk about themselves, and show how much they knew about their local history. Especially when someone attractive asked the questions.

We must have filled at least a quarter of every episode with stories we picked up this way.

"What did he tell you about the ghostly bluesman?" I asked, using the term we'd been given with the directions.

"Never heard of it," she said, but dismissively. Like that wasn't the important part.

Then she continued, and we all saw why.

"He told me about a little cemetery out here." Page leaned forward a little more. "Said it has a *vampire*."

All three of us repeated that word.

Me, with surprise.

Tangi, with hopeful disbelief.

Todd, with scorn.

"Come on," Todd said a moment later. "The evidence of actual physical vampires is so scant—"

"Which do you want to come back with," Page said. "Clips of nothing and barely enough local lore to fill one segment, let alone a whole show?"

She smiled wider. The smile I thought we should have put on all our posters.

"Or a decrepit cemetery that's supposed to house a vampire?"

"Vampire," I said, not missing a beat.

"Vampire," Tangi agreed. "Make great television."

"I don't know," Todd said. "Think about our reputations."

"We're supposed to pursue all kinds of paranormal phenomena," Page said, "but we're just known for ghosts right now. Like a thousand other shows. But if we give the public *one good* show about a site that even *might* be a vampire?"

"She's right, Todd," I said.

Tangi nodded.

Todd rubbed his chin. Worked his lips around.

"All right," he said, "but we do this by the book. Pure science. None of this superstitious mumbo jumbo."

"Please," Page said, sounding more offended than she looked. She had a getting-away-with-something glint in her eye. "It'll even give us an excuse to break out the vampire hunting equipment. And you *know* that'll get us viewers, plus draw attention to the science of what we're doing."

That put a smile on Todd's face.

THE DRIVE TO THE CEMETERY WAS, IF ANYTHING, WORSE THAN THE drive to those crossroads.

Not because of Todd. He was doing much better now. Sitting in the back and chattering with Page about vampires, while Tangi read off the directions Page had scribbled down following her earlier chat with the gas station attendant.

Not even because we'd had to spend a good hour-plus just getting back to the gas shed, so we could start to follow those directions.

No, the problem was that some of the excuses for roads I drove down had been almost washed out by flash storms. Had to off-road here and there in a vehicle *so* not made for it.

I swear, I don't think I ever got the speedometer past fifteen on the whole drive.

Plus, a couple of times, Tangi and I had to get out and un-stick the van from a patch of mud.

Didn't do much for my state of mind.

Not to mention the extra backtracking to find landmarks, because the directions included lines like "take a left when you come to the stump that looks like Dwight Eisenhower."

Took us three tries before we found a stump that we agreed looked vaguely like an ex-president. Though I thought it looked more like Gerald Ford than Eisenhower.

Finally, though, we were there.

We were used to late nights, but even the four of us were yawning as we piled out of the van once more.

After way too much time on bumpy dirt roads, while consuming enough caffeine to hold us together, all of us needed to find a place to relieve ourselves.

Page was the most urgent of us, and the only one who had to do it by herself, so she got to shuffle off to a convenient tree first, while the other three of us hung out discreetly on the other side of the van until she was done.

I'd already run more sound checks than I needed for the equipment, so after a quick check of my battery life (fine), I started setting up mics and getting levels.

Funny thing about this place. It sounded dead.

I mean, the last place was overflowing with crickets, frogs, cicadas and whatnot. But this place, it was like they'd all suddenly found appointments elsewhere and took off.

Not even the cry of a night bird while I was setting up.

I might have found it creepy, but I wrote it off. After all, I was a city boy — or at least a suburb boy — at heart, and for all I knew the insects and frogs packed it in for the night not long after midnight.

I did get a good look at the place while the others were taking their turns on the other side of the van.

The cemetery itself was a sad little thing. Neglected and forgotten for far too long. *Maybe* fifteen graves in three rows of five, and all of them overgrown with wild grass, except for one spot in the back.

The grave markers — the ones still standing I mean — weren't more than raw wood. None of them still even looked like crosses. Just little rounded stakes of wood, weather-worn long past the point of legibility.

And we tried, once Tangi turned the lights on. Not one of them had two letters we could put together. Tangi took plenty of pictures, though, in case he could do something in the lab to help their legibility.

Around the cemetery was a fence that wasn't in any better shape than the grave markers. Looked like it might have been white once, and tall as my waist. But half of it had collapsed, most of the rest was moss-covered and raw.

The gate, if there ever was one, was long gone.

Surrounding the fence were little yellow flowers. Two breeds. I couldn't pick them out, but Todd declared them black-eyed Susans and primroses, the moment he came back around the van.

They might have been neat rows of flowers once. Now, of course, they were strewn with weeds, and just as sad as the grave markers.

Behind the cemetery started a small wood. Mostly oaks, I thought, which made me smile because those were one of the few types of trees I could pick out. And whatever the others were, I knew they weren't elms.

Todd said they were dogwoods. I took his word for it.

I took my turn on the other side of the van, and by the time I was done dropping what felt like a half-gallon, Tangi already had the lights up and was taking still shots.

I walked up to where Todd and Page were talking quietly.

"How do you want to do this?" I asked. "Usual I.R. scope shots after we get our atmosphere?"

"No," Page said, and she was smiling the way she usually didn't. Like she was getting a treat of some kind. "No, you and Tangi get to be on camera tonight."

"Nobody wants to see us," I said. "They want to see the hotties. You two."

"They will," Todd said, smiling just as wide. I tried to tell myself it wasn't because he knew I never felt comfortable on camera. "But you and Tangi need to be armed, so you need to be in shots too."

"But..."

I didn't bother finishing the sentence. I saw the determined gleam in Page's eye.

"Each of us goes armed," she said, in a tone that brooked no defiance. And that was a tone she did well. "I mean it. I doubt we'll meet a vampire, but if we do, I want us ready."

"Besides," Todd said, voice awfully teasing for a guy who was on the edge of a beating not all that long ago, "aren't you the one who says we let our equipment go to waste too often? Aren't you the one who insists the tech makes good television?"

"No," Tangi said, smiling as he joined us. "That's me. But I like that you remembered."

"Right," Page said. "Weapon up. Then we'll take some stalking shots. Us through the woods, like we're hunting the vampire. Then we'll find the grave and start doing the more serious stuff."

Page meant that. But she couldn't have had any idea how right she was.

STALKING SHOTS WERE OLD HAT TO US. THEY DIDN'T WORK FOR EVERY haunting, but that just made them more effective when we got to use them.

First, we donned our night vision goggles. Then Tangi went to the infrared camera. Not only did that cover a multitude of sins that would have shown up under bright lights and full-spectrum shots — fast food wrappers hanging out of a pocket, for example — but it also lent everything an eerie, otherworldly look.

Then Page and Todd led the way through some patch of woods or other — a little stretch of road this time, too, since they had a cemetery to approach. Filmed in IR with lots of ambient sound, it would do good things for tension.

In that way, the lack of woodland creatures — and annoying insects — was good for our filming. Let Todd and Page remark in harsh whispers about the "unnatural quiet." And I was pretty sure they meant it.

Me, I just figured it was some combination of the extremely late hour with the odd weather patterns.

Either way, the silence meant we could record Page and Todd whispering here and there, instead of talking. And my mics picked up every rustle of leaves and snap of a twig.

This was going to make great television.

Especially once we had the voice over in place. Little bits of discussion about the history of the place, maybe vampires in general for this one.

Page and Todd had lots of theories about vampires. But then, they had lots of theories about everything.

Our stalking shots would look even better this time, with the weapons. Like we really were hunting.

Todd carried an ultraviolet light that could put out something like a hundred thousand lumens. Needed both hands to carry it, but it could, in theory, flash fry a vampire in seconds.

Made us all glad that Page designed our goggles to guard against U.V., even as they showed us infrared. Just in case Todd panicked and fired that thing off.

Page had two weapons, one in each hand. A smaller U.V. lamp — maybe fifty thousand lumens — plus a Colt .45 loaded with wooden bullets.

Page's designs, of course. Everything we were carrying. Used to be I'd ask about exactly how many electrical engineering classes she'd taken, but she never gave me a solid answer.

Electrical engineering, though, wouldn't help her design bullets. And I really had to hope she knew what she was doing on that score. Tangi and I were both carrying shotguns with wooden pellets in the shells.

Focusing on my mics was the only thing that kept me from imagining the gun blowing up in my face because she'd screwed up the shotgun shells.

Finally, though, we got all the setup shots.

Now, all four of us stood over that dead patch of grass, near the back-right corner of the cemetery.

Page was speaking into Tangi's handheld camera.

"Notice the dead grass here. In some parts of eastern Europe, it's said that nothing can grow above a vampire's grave."

She waved her hand over some broken mason jars. Blue glass, with tin lids, and some stuff still inside them.

Despite what Page just said, those jars were how she knew we had the right grave. The cashier at that gas station had insisted that those broken mason jars were Ozark folk magic, for keeping a vampire from your door.

"Notice what we can see inside the jars," Page said. "Oil, at least two varieties, plus crushed and ground herbs, and bits of cloth or ribbon. Now, from my own studies of Ozark folk magic those would indicate—"

"What's this?"

Something cold washed down my body at the sound of those two words. Partially because they hadn't been spoken by any of us, and I couldn't believe that anyone just happened to come walking through here, with the sky just starting to gray toward dawn.

The other reason? The voice of the speaker was rough with

disuse. Almost like his throat had forgotten how to talk, and he was reminding it right now.

All four of us turned at once.

The speaker didn't look like much, to be honest. Just a local yokel, as we called them. Greasy black hair. Unwashed. Maybe a couple inches over five foot nothing, and he couldn't have weighed a buck and a half. He was wearing torn jeans that looked older than I was, and the kind of flannel shirt that was supposed to be more common in the Pacific Northwest than in rural Missouri.

And he wasn't even wearing it over a tee shirt. And with a belly like his, he should have kept it covered.

All of that I took in within a quick glance.

Because it took my mind exactly that long to realize why my balls had just tried to crawl up inside my body, while my bladder was begging for another evacuation, and my stomach was trying to jump ship and head for the hills.

We were looking at the world through IR goggles.

And this guy, he was cold.

Not dead-tree-limb cold. That might have been worse. But humans, under IR they glow more than a little. This guy, he only glowed a little. From that big belly, mostly.

He was too cold to be a living man. Even if he was too warm to be a corpse.

"I beg your—" Todd started.

He never got that fourth word out.

The little guy grabbed Todd and slashed open our pretty boy's throat.

Blood gushed hot and bright into the night air. But the little guy, he wasn't letting it go to waste.

He clamped his mouth over the wound and starting glowing warmer in my night vision goggles as Todd's lifeblood went swallowing down the other's throat.

No. Not "other." I knew what the word for this guy was, even if I didn't want to think it. Even if my mind didn't want to admit the truth.

The little guy was a vampire.

All three of us were frozen in horror at the scene playing out before us.

Page came to her senses first.

"Light him up!" she screamed.

Page hit her UV light and opened fire with her pistol.

I dropped my mic and opened up with my shotgun.

Tangi dropped his camera and let fly with his own shotgun.

Three sets of wooden bullets — well, one set of bullets and two sets of shotgun shot — slammed into the vampire's chest. Not to mention Page hitting it with some fifty thousand lumens of ultraviolet light.

And the vampire didn't even notice.

He finished sucking Todd dry, then threw — physically flung — Todd's body at me. Slammed it into me.

Both me and Todd's corpse went flying.

I could hear Page screaming before I even hit the ground.

Then my head hit a rock, and the world was a dizzy, painful place.

I tried to get up, but my arms weren't working right. My legs, either. Everything was too wobbly. And the world was spinning. Couldn't get up.

I couldn't hear much but the blood rushing past my ears.

My head hurt so bad, I rolled over and retched up everything I'd eaten in the last nine hours onto the thick grass at the foot of one of Todd's dogwood trees.

By the time I rolled my pasty, sweaty self back over, everything was too quiet. Between painful throbs of my head, I tried to figure out what that meant.

I was afraid I knew already.

I didn't have my shotgun. Where was my shotgun?

Suddenly the vampire was standing over me.

I could see him now, in the slowly lightening gray of pre-dawn. My night vision goggles must have gotten knocked off in the fall.

His skin was ruddy, not pale. His black curls hung limp and unwashed down to his shoulders.

He was covered in blood. And smiling.

"Wooden bullets?" he said, then chuckled. His voice still sounded rusty, but a lot smoother now. Like either he was getting better at remembering how to talk, or his meal had helped.

And he was still talking.

"Ultraviolet light?" He shook his head. "How can you study so much, but learn so little?"

He reached for me then, and everything went black.

2

<hr>

Lots of little things that I couldn't comprehend at the time.

Lights, but no sound. Just glows of white. Some bright. Some dim. Occasionally tinged with yellow or blue, but most often just white light.

Other times it was sound, but no light. Voices, talking in harsh whispers, or echoing conversation. Either way, I couldn't make heads or tails of what they were saying.

I did hear beeping, but it could have been someone's alarm clock or a truck backing up, for all the sense it made to me.

I think I tried to speak during that weird period. I'm pretty sure I tried to move, too.

I didn't have any success at either.

There were smells, but none of them were pleasant. Some of them were the worst kinds of human smells. Others were the worst kinds of cleaning smells.

It was the smells that let me know that I was, in fact, alive. I hadn't been sure for a while there.

Some afterworlds might have had me smelling dung or urine, but not in any version of heaven or hell did I ever hear about anyone smelling bleach.

Finally, though, my eyes opened, and some of those lights began to resolve themselves into a hospital room.

Lots of white, but some attempt at blue too. Like the room had originally been all white, from the linoleum flooring to the walls and trim, to the acoustic ceiling tiles. But somewhere along the line, someone must have decided that a soothing blue would have been better. So they got the room painted pale blue with white trim.

But they must not have enough in the budget for more than one coat, or they must not have maintained it right.

Now it just looked like bluish white that made me want to be sick.

The bed was the usual kind of hospital fare I'd known from college football injuries. Stiff, and narrow, but with mechanical controls to raise it and lower it, plus a roller table, and sidebars that could come up in case they thought I needed restraints.

Apparently I did, because they were up now.

I had an IV too, but it just looked like saline to me.

I could move a bit, but my arms and legs felt like they'd been filled with lead.

Across the room, I could see a little white board. Said the duty nurse's name was Jeffries.

Jeffries.

Todd's last name was Jeffries.

I started crying then. I thought it was just quiet tears, but someone must have heard me. I hadn't been crying for more than a minute before the door flew open and people started pouring into the room.

The first in was my nurse, a big, heavy, square-jawed guy who looked like he should have had a thick beard, tattoos and nose rings, but had none of them. The only thing that fit his size and rough-and-tumble look was the close-cropped hair.

Piling in after him were two uniformed cops. One of them already had his hand on his gun.

The gun was a revolver. Thirty-eight, if I had to guess, and I was pretty sure I didn't want to find out.

The cop with his hand on it didn't look much bigger than his gun.

Skinny. The kind of guy whose Adam's apple stuck out almost a foot, and had the beak to go with it. Add in the pallor, and I wondered how this guy made it through their physical training.

Must have been hella tenacious. Had that look in his eyes, and those eyes were trained on me.

The nurse reached me first, one hand on my wrist, the other on my forehead. He was asking questions, but all my wide-eyed attention was on one cop's hand, gripping the handle of his pistol.

"Johnson," the other cop growled. "Get me coffee. Now."

"But—"

"Now."

The skinny cop turned and left. The nurse turned to the remaining cop. Said, "He's not going anywhere. Does this have to be done now? Mr. Robertson here has been through—"

"Lives hang in the balance."

I was starting to think this other cop always growled. Must have been a lot of fun to be this guy's wife. If he asked for orange juice or the newspaper, he probably sounded like he was accusing her of treason.

And he *was* married. Saw the ring on his beefy finger. Not hard to spot, since he only had the one arm. The other arm stopped just above the elbow, with his shirt sleeve pinned up over the end.

He was in good shape, otherwise. Much more the kind of lean, fit build I was used to from California cops. At least, the ones I'd run into.

Then again, I didn't know what state I was in. That just made me sweat harder as I continued looking over the cop.

He hadn't shaved today, and the hair under his hat was as high and tight as my nurse's.

And my nurse was still talking.

"At least let me—"

"Out," the cop said. "You can tend to that later."

"He's *my* patient," Nurse ... my nurse said.

"And right now he's *my* prisoner. Don't think you want to be charged with obstructing justice."

The nurse and cop tried to stare one another down.

The cop won.

"This is going in my report," my nurse said, "and our administration will talk to your superiors."

"And if I save one life not waiting another damned minute for my information, I won't give a fuck who says what about it. Now *out!*"

The moment the nurse was out of the room, and the door closed — and locked, I noted — the cop turned a much more pleasant demeanor to me.

"Relax, son," he said, taking off his hat. The gesture might have been friendlier, if his voice didn't sound like he was accusing me of murder. "You're not really under arrest. But I need information from you, and I need it now."

"I..." Anything else I might have thought of saying was lost in a coughing jag.

"Easy there," the cop said. "You lost a lot of blood, and they say your throat was pretty raw. Gonna have a hell of a scar. And that doesn't take into account the concussion. You're lucky to be alive."

He handed me a cup of ice chips. It was shaky in my unsteady hand, but I managed to keep it upright while the cop squirted water into it from a squirt bottle.

He took the cup back and held it up for me to sip from the straw as he talked a little more.

"My name is Officer John Reynolds," he said. "You're at Springfield General Hospital in Springfield, Missouri. And I need you to get your voice as fast as possible. Can you do that for me?"

The ice water felt like heaven itself, flowing down my throat. I sipped a little more, surprised at just how dry my mouth was, before I nodded.

"Good," Officer Reynolds said. "Good."

"How long..." I couldn't quite finish the question, but he answered it anyway as he gave me some more water.

"Three days. First time you've been really conscious, which is why I'm pushing. Given a choice, son, I'd love to let you get your strength back and feel one hundred percent before I ask you what happened. But we're up against it, and every minute counts."

I shook my head.

"You don't remember?"

"I don't want to," I admitted.

"I get that," he said, and he almost sounded soothing. "I do. Last thing *I* ever want to think about is the night I lost my arm. But, son, some of your friends might still be alive. All right?"

"Really? I mean, Todd—"

"Todd Jeffries is dead," Officer Reynolds said, and that sentence came out downright gentle. Got back to his more normal tone as he continued though. "I hate to be the one to remind you, but something tore his head clean off. Maybe the same animal that got hold of you."

"Wasn't an animal," I said, shaking my head. "It was a man."

"There we go," Officer Reynolds was trying to keep the excitement out of his voice, but he couldn't manage it. He did set the cup down and whip out a crumpled notebook and pen. Balanced the notebook on his knee with practiced ease as he started taking notes. "That's right. The animals had to have a handler. Tell me everything you can."

I described the vampire as much as I could. I didn't use the word "vampire" though. I just didn't say anything about any kind of animal, either.

"All right," Officer Reynolds said, then lost a moment when an insistent knock started. He hustled over, took a cup of coffee, and shooed the other cop away.

"Sorry about that," Officer Reynolds said, when he returned, putting his coffee down on the table. "About that idiot putting his hand on his gun, too. He had this damned fool theory that you were behind it."

He shook his head. "Rookies."

"What about Page?" I asked. "And Tangi?"

"Well, that's just it," Officer Reynolds said. "They're missing."

I NEEDED A MOMENT — AND MORE ICE WATER FROM MY CUP — BEFORE I could begin to process that.

Tangi and Page were missing?

But ... I heard her scream. Like she was dying. And I knew there was no way the vampire could have attacked Page without Tangi getting between them.

Missing. That just made no sense.

"What do you mean?" I said, at last.

"I mean we found a lot of blood. More than one human being could hold. And we found ... *one* of your friends. But Tangi Maaka and Page Carmichael were nowhere to be found."

Officer Reynolds leaned in to give me a compassionate gaze. "And believe me, son, we looked."

I nodded.

"Now," Officer Reynolds said, easing back in the visitor's chair a little and taking up his pen again. "I know it wasn't a bear that ripped into you guys, and I know you were carrying some pretty strange weaponry. Wooden dum-dum rounds? UV lights? Just what kind of exotic animal were you hunting?"

"It wasn't an animal," I started but Officer Reynolds held up his hand to interrupt me.

"Come clean, son," he said. "I'm not here about exotic animal permits, and I'm not here about hunting licenses. Once we find your friends, those things may matter and they may not. Especially if you can help us bring in a ring of poachers."

"Poachers?"

"Where did you think the critters come from, son?" Officer Reynolds gave me a men-of-the-world look. "Poachers nab them from other countries, and they sneak them into ours. Then they take them out into the middle of nowhere, where Hollywood types like yourselves pay top dollar to hunt them."

"That's not what—"

"What I don't get," Officer Reynolds said, "is why you were only trying to distract or stun it. Was that a cost thing? So much to hunt it, but so much more to kill it?"

"But that's not what—"

"Son, the clock is ticking here," he said, sitting forward now. "Whatever happened out there, your contacts spooked and split. And they took your friends with them."

Officer Reynolds reached out and put his hand on my arm.

"Cooperate with me, son. Give me the name and information of your contact. Everything you know. We need to nab them before the ransom demands begin, or the feds will take it over. I can't help you then."

"Help me?"

"Of course," he said, sitting back and taking up his pen again. "I'm just a state cop, but I have the power to make sure the state's attorney knows you cooperated with us entirely, and helped us bring in the poachers and lock them away."

"But—"

"You and me, son," he said, tapping the pen urgently. "You and me can keep this from ever happening to anyone else."

"But—"

"Think before you speak, son," he said, gruff voice urgent now. "No one else has to die like your friend Todd. No one else has to get kidnapped at gunpoint like your friends Tan-gi and Page."

He patted my wrist. "Help me now. We can save your friends. Get the bad guys. And we can keep you out of jail. But you have to help me now."

"But, Officer," I tried, but Officer Reynolds clucked his tongue.

"Don't do it, Selwyn. Don't you just give me a story. That could lead to all your friends being dead. The poachers getting away. And you seeing the inside of a jail cell for a long, long time."

"*Listen to me,*" I said.

"Son," Officer Reynolds said, "I don't want to do anything else."

"Did you see our van? Did you see the logo? The camera equipment?"

"Yeah, I saw them." He nodded. "Your little show. Good cover. Means you can go anywhere, and most people won't turn an eye."

"Everyone turns an eye," I said. "We want them to. We don't set foot in a city where we don't interview a dozen people. Where we don't try to grab all the attention we can."

"What are you trying to tell me, son? That you just *happened* on a poacher hunt? Is that it? Is that why they kidnapped your friends?"

"There were no poachers!"

I was breathing hard now. Sweating out every drop I'd drunk and everything the IV had pumped into me. My mouth was dry again, and my heart was pounding so hard that the world was turning red on me.

But I finally had the cop's attention.

"Look," I said. "We weren't out there hunting any animals, exotic or otherwise. And we didn't run across a poacher. We'd been out at an old crossroads, looking for the ghost of a bluesman who didn't show up. For our show."

"You were found nowhere near a crossroads."

"No. *Earlier.* The crossroads was the reason we were out there. Check the footage."

That got me a guarded look from Officer Reynolds.

"We didn't find any footage, son. Did you even shoot any?"

"Hell yes! Hours worth! I recorded more damned crickets and cicadas than—"

"All right, all right," Officer Reynolds said, waving his pen like a white flag. "Let's play it your way for now. Maybe the poachers erased your footage. Maybe they stole it. Let's get back to your crossroads. What did you do when the ghost didn't show?"

"Page lost her shit. Said it was a snipe hunt, but that she'd heard about a little cemetery with a vampire."

"Vampire?" Officer Reynolds asked. And he managed to drip so much sarcasm into his tone that I noticed it, and I'd long since stopped noticing the sarcasm people gave me about our show.

"Vampire," I said. "We didn't expect to find one, of course," I said, knowing full well that half of us did indeed expect that finding a vampire was a possibility. "But we had a show to put on, so we wanted it to look good for the camera."

"Wooden bullets. UV lamps." Officer Reynolds rubbed his chin. "Might be you're telling me the truth."

"I *am* telling you the truth."

"Then you had the weapons just for show?"

Looking back now, I think I was just too upset and too exhausted and drained to see the trap.

"Yeah," I said, starting to wilt. I just didn't have the energy to stay that agitated. "Page wanted us to carry them, but really it was just so they'd look good on camera."

"So," Officer Reynolds said slowly, face neutral but eyes sharp, "why'd you fire the shotgun?"

"Why—" I tried, but he cut me off.

"You fired a shotgun. We found the gun. Found the powder burns. Yadda yadda yadda. Don't think just 'cause we're in a flyover state that we don't know our business."

"I never thought that," I said, in complete honesty.

In fact, enough honesty in my voice that Officer Reynolds eased down a little.

"So," he said, a little more gently. "What was it you fired at? What was it, ripped off Todd Jeffries head? Really."

"I told you," I said. "It was a man. And I fired right into his chest, near point blank range. So did Tangi. So did Page."

"All three of you? What were the other two shooting?"

Figured that might have been a test, but I didn't care. I told him all about our weapons.

"Even wooden bullets would have stopped a human," Officer Reynolds said, shaking his head. "Especially if he was on the skinny side, with a bit of a paunch. Sure you hit him?"

"Positive. All three of us hit him."

"So why didn't I find his body? Alive or dead? Why didn't I find a trail of blood I couldn't at least type match to you and your friends?"

"Because we didn't even slow him down. None of it did." A chill ran through me. Shivered me so hard the bed shook.

"That vampire's still out there, Officer. And you're telling me he has my friends."

THE CONVERSATION PRETTY MUCH WENT SOUTH AT THAT POINT.

I was fixated on the vampire, and on what had happened to Page and Tangi.

Officer Reynolds, he was pretty sure I was lying to cover my ass and stay out of jail.

In some ways, it was a good thing that I physically couldn't leave the hospital. Turned out that the hospital administration had, indeed, complained to the state police about how things were being handled. The cops weren't even allowed to talk to me again for several days.

During those days, Officer Reynolds and his rookie partner had been quite busy. They'd dug just about as heavily into my past as it was possible to go. Not to mention Todd's past, and Page's, and Tangi's, and the whole show.

In fact, from what he told me the next time I saw him, Officer Reynolds actually called all over the country, contacting people who'd been interviewed on our show. Pretty much anyone who'd ever been in touch with us.

But he could have saved all that time. Because he'd actually made the most important phone call on that first day after he talked to me.

He'd called our producers.

So had Page, as it turned out.

While I'd been struggling with the backroads of Missouri after that snipe hunt at the crossroads, Page had gotten on the phone to everyone associated with the show that she could think of. I suspect she'd just been trying to wake people up. Make them suffer just a little, for all the suffering they'd given us on this trip.

Not that she had any idea what...

Anyway, point is she'd told no less than a dozen people at the network where we were, what we were doing, and why.

And every second of that was recorded on voice mail, and time and date stamped.

I think she even sent emails. Page was thorough at the best of times, and when she was angry, she was even more of a stickler.

Even the attendant at the gas station talked to the cops about his conversation with the beautiful Page Carmichael, and how he hoped the vampire didn't get her.

So everything about my story that could have been corroborated, was corroborated.

Everything but the lack of footage. But as the evidence piled up that we had, in truth, been out there filming an episode of *Seekers*, the lack of footage looked more and more like an indicator of foul play.

In fact, the next time I saw Officer Reynolds, it was so he could apologize for "antagonizing" me — obviously not his choice of words — and that he was sorry for my loss.

Not just over Todd, either. Page and Tangi were still missing, and since it had been about a week, the cops weren't hopeful of ever finding them.

Me, I was pretty sure no one would ever find them. I was pretty sure they'd been late-morning snacks for that vampire.

I even confessed as much. I mean, I was in it that far anyway. Might as well try to get people to listen to the truth.

After all, Page, Todd, and Tangi had died trying to find the truth and bring it to the public. How could I do any less to honor their memories?

I'll tell you how.

I got locked up.

Not in jail. Oh, no. That might have led to the wrong kind of questions. That might have been something I could fight.

No, they slapped me with a psych eval. Possibly a fifty-one-fifty. Not sure about that. I know I heard the words "trauma," "psychotic episode," "schizoid episode," "hallucination," and a few other choice terms, over the course of the following few weeks.

I went right out of one kind of hospital and into another. And I was declared a danger to myself and others. After all, I'd been carrying deadly weapons with the intention of shooting a "vampire" and had, in fact shot a weapon at another human being I'd believed to be a "vampire."

That fact that this "person" couldn't be found didn't matter. The fact that no one but me believed that this "person" even existed didn't matter.

What mattered was what it meant.

As a danger to myself and others, I could be committed against my will.

My family was notified, at least. They were able to get me transferred from the public facility in Missouri to a private facility in California.

That was both good and bad.

It was good in that the place was much nicer. Better food, better accommodations, nicer people, and a pleasant environment to walk around in.

It had a shaded pond. And ducks.

I even got visits from my mom and dad, though those were both good and bad. I was happy to see them, but those sad, worried expressions I could have done without.

My sister didn't come to visit. Mom said Tina just couldn't handle seeing me "like this."

Yeah, that was the start of the bad side.

The worst of the bad side was that these doctors were too sharp to fool.

See, I'd figured out pretty quickly that my only way out of this mess was to tell them that it wasn't really a vampire that killed my friends. I was even coming up with some pretty convincing lies to cover up.

Figured I'd get out, then get back to the truth and maybe see about hunting down that vampire.

Not to mention hunting down the reason I was left alive, while my friends were killed.

That was a question that kept me up nights in a cold sweat. And I think that question was probably the key to the doctors all seeing right through my lies.

They knew I wasn't telling the truth about what happened. No matter what story I told. No matter how I told it.

They knew. And they weren't going to let me go. Not until I sounded just as sure as they were that I hadn't seen anything like a vampire.

They weren't going to pretend they knew what happened to my friends. The doctors even confessed that I might never admit the truth to myself. But they could not let me go until I released the delusion that I was under.

That was all. That one thing. They were convinced that my break had been relatively minor, and temporary. That they were sure I was ready to return to society, an upstanding member. Ready to continue a normal life.

Ready ... except for that one detail.

Because until I was willing to admit "the truth" to myself, that little hole in my psyche was just waiting for someone or something to happen and blow it wide open.

The doctors, they weren't willing to release me. Not while that hole was just waiting for the wrong stimulus.

And so they tried drugs.

They tried psychotherapy.

They tried group therapy.

They tried a great many things.

I fought them at first. Felt I owed it to Page, Todd and Tangi to hold onto the truth. The truth they'd died for.

But as weeks passed, as the doctors went about their business, there was only so hard I could grip that little nugget of belief.

That certainty that I could trust my own memory of events.

It *had* been a traumatic night, after all. Even before we got to the cemetery.

And whatever happened to me there, it *had* been too much for any one person to stand, and still call himself sane. It was too much.

And that didn't take into account my blood loss. My blow to the head. No. Not just a blow to the head. A *concussion*.

All of it happened right when we all had vampires on the brain, for the show. Had just spent an hour or two focused on vampires, finding "evidence" of vampires.

Not to mention, of course, the elephant in the room — I had been left alive.

Eventually, I couldn't help but wonder — were the doctors right?

3

FIVE YEARS.

That's how long it took for the doctors to convince me that their version of reality — that I'd suffered a psychotic break — was correct.

Well, I think they'd had me convinced inside of three, maybe three-and-a-half years. But it was five years before their corrections to my thinking truly took, and I understood to the core of my being that I had not, in fact faced a vampire.

No, the doctors didn't know what happened that night.

We'd tried regression therapy. With two or three different therapists and approaches, including something called the Kritzendorf Distancing Technique.

None of them had done any good.

Every time I relived that night, I relived the experience, just the way I remembered it.

Delusion. I relived the *delusion* just the way I remembered it.

That saddened the doctors, but ultimately they decided that I was healthy enough to make my way in the world once more, without any realistic threat to myself and others.

Or, at least, no *more* of a threat to myself and others than any other member of society.

After all, to hear the doctors tell it, we're all crazy. The only question is the *degree* of crazy, and whether or not our crazy impeded our ability to function in the civilized world.

Or maybe it was one of the other patients who told me that.

Either way, just about five years even after the night of my "keystone event" — not a formal psych term, I think, but what my regression therapists kept calling that night in Missouri — I was walking out of the facility a free man.

A free man, with an actual certificate of sanity. Didn't know how many other people could honestly claim they were *certifiably* sane.

Anyway, from there, I spent a little time with my folks. Couple of months. Getting to know them again, and maybe reassuring them that I was still their son. Not sure how well I got that across. They were on eggshells the whole time.

Tina actually even came by a few times, while I was there.

Still skittish around me, which hurt. Kept staring at the jagged scar across the left side of my throat.

Couldn't blame her though. She'd always been my baby sister. So clever, but so fragile, and fine-boned. I'd always protected her.

And now I'd been damaged. Couldn't even protect myself...

Stop.

That wasn't the right direction for my thoughts. The doctors told me to try to avoid shaming myself over what happened that night. It was beyond my control.

I wasn't at fault for Todd's death. Or Page and Tangi's disappearances.

Their bodies had never been found, of course.

Probably devoured by whatever exotic animal we'd run across. No way of knowing, really.

I didn't sponge off my folks for long.

I pulled myself together and got back to work. Not on a paranormal television show, of course. The time for those had passed. And besides, there was no way I wanted to come near anything "paranormal" ever again.

No, I found a nice, simple little documentary company outside of

Sacramento that produced thirty, sixty, ninety, and hundred-and-twenty minute films about things like the environment, different species of wildlife, and other innocent topics that weren't likely to lead me down any dark roads.

I avoided the political documentaries for just that reason. Never knew where politics would lead.

But doing sound for dolphins and big cats and baby harp seals? Yeah, that I could handle.

And I was still good enough at sound work that I could almost pick my gig. Truth was, I had offers from some of the big movie studios down south, to run sound for them.

I turned them all down flat though. Going near Hollywood would only have encouraged the Vultures.

That was what I called them, anyway. They were about a step below paparazzi. The Vultures were the ones desperate to get me on camera again. To feed into my old delusion, all so they could get money out of "telling my story" to a public that "needs to know."

After I broke the first one's nose — on the street outside my parent's place, not two days after I got out — they actually called the cops.

The cops told them to fuck off. Possibly in so many words. One of the nice side effects of coming from a rich family in a small community north of San Francisco like Santa Marina, was that the police tended to side with us locals on pretty much everything.

Then my dad's lawyers started barking at the Vultures, and they stopped circling altogether.

Oh, not entirely. They were still there now and then. But they didn't come close. Dad's lawyers made it clear that I was too risky to go after.

And worse than risky, I was boring to their editors now.

I'd moved into an apartment in Rancho Verde, a one-movie-theater town outside of Sacramento. Making my money doing sound for a little company's nature films.

That kind of thing was death to the Vultures. No prayer of a scandal.

But if I'd gone south of Monterey again, they'd probably have descended on me in flocks, leading with their mics and their cameras firing nonstop.

I wasn't going to give them a chance.

I just showed up at the office every day, and ran my mics and mixers. Once in a great while, when it wasn't too inconvenient, I'd be willing to go out on location for them. So long as it was someplace secluded, and *all the filming happened during the day.*

Nighttime.

That was one little detail I'd managed to hide from the doctors. Or maybe I hadn't. Maybe they knew, but they didn't care because it didn't stop me from functioning.

But nighttime still scared the hell out of me.

I never wanted to be outside my own home after sunset. And I moved heaven and earth to avoid it.

So, yeah, the studio owners thought my hours were weird, but they didn't care. Not really. So long as I hit every deadline, I could come and go as I pleased.

My chosen schedule meant I didn't date at all. And I didn't go to a whole lot of social events. But I just didn't care about any of those things.

Not enough to risk going out at night.

Three years, I lived that way.

Three years of punching the clock and making documentaries.

Three years of hiding from what, deep down, I'd always known was the truth.

Three years until one man brought it all crashing back down on me.

4

It was another hot day. A Saturday in July.

But here in Rancho Verde, we got a dry heat. Not Arizona dry, but still. Dry enough that even when the it pushed a hundred — as it would later that day — it never felt so bad to me.

It was my day off, but I didn't sleep in. I never did. Not anymore.

My need to be home by sunset meant life was easier if I got up nice and early every morning. Generally about fifteen minutes before sunrise, which would give me time to move around a bit before stepping outside to get my morning paper.

Yes, I still got the morning paper.

Anyway, the paper would wait that morning. And so would my shower.

My days off always started with a good, long run.

Running was something I never really got to do while I was ... in that facility. They had space, but not enough. And I got bored lapping the same level green grass and pond and peach-colored buildings, inside those high, stone, peach-colored walls.

Here, I could pick my routes. When I felt like going through the steady suburban streets, I did. When I felt like running down by the riverfront, I did that instead.

I had options.

I never ran the same route twice in a row. Never fell into any kind of pattern.

That morning it was the riverfront. The river ran all the way through Rancho Verde, which gave me more than five miles one way, if I wanted to run it from my place to the edge of town.

On a cooler day, I might have done it. But even shortly after dawn it was already in the high seventies. Figured I'd just run until my body told me it was time to head back.

I took my break early for me. Only three, maybe three-and-a-half miles in. Just dropped down onto the grass near the river, watching a pair of other early risers — a happy couple in their twenties, if I was any judge — play some complicated game involving their three dogs and two Frisbees.

The thick grass by the river, though, it felt good on my bare back. I was only wearing my running shoes and a pair of basketball shorts. Blue and gold for the Warriors, of course.

Birds were singing in a nearby elm tree.

I was hot, and sweaty, but my muscles had that good runner vibe going, and with a bucolic scene like that around me, I was feeling pretty darned good.

Right up until I heard my name.

"Mr. Robertson?"

I was on my feet, fists clenched. Just that fast.

The guy I was squaring off with immediately put up his hands in surrender. And I had to admit, he didn't look like a Vulture.

He was taller than me. Must have been pushing six-and-a-half feet. And he had the kind of slender frame that probably stayed skinny without an ounce of effort on his part.

He was pale, with a reddish tint to his skin, highlighted by his thin, neatly trimmed silver hair.

Fine, small features, but long fingers on his hands.

Neatly manicured fingers...

Usually meant a guy thought a lot of himself, if he put that much trouble into getting his fingernails looking that neat and clean.

This was something I picked up in the hospital. The therapists I hated were the ones most fastidious about their appearance. They were the kind of sticklers who thought every little variation in my grammar and intonation could tell them *deep things* about my psyche.

This guy reminded me of them.

The blue silk suit, lavender tie, and shiny black shoes didn't help him.

"You *are* Selwyn Robertson?" he said, and this time I noted his accent. Not regional, but educated. Precise. Like ivy league, or maybe an English university. But if the latter, he didn't sound like a native son from across the pond.

I gave him a grudging nod, but not a smile. "Just who the fuck are you?"

He blinked owlish gray eyes at me.

"Apparently I must apologize," he said with an actual bow. This guy's posture could have been featured in instructional videos. "Please forgive me if I have given offense. That was never my intention."

"Who *are* you?"

"Oh, dear," he said, and his brow creased in a frown that didn't quite reach his lips. "I was so hoping that approaching you openly in a public place might see you in a better mood. I don't know every-thing, I'm afraid, no matter what anyone tells you."

This time I raised my fists. Not high enough for a threat. Not just yet. But just high enough to make his eyes notice them again.

"I'm not going to ask again, pal."

"Oh, I've handled this all wrong. I'm so sorry." He somehow managed to draw himself even straighter and taller, shoulders back and head held high. "My name is Edmund Xerxes. And I must speak with you."

Xerxes. Why did I know that name?

I mean, yeah, there were the Greek references, but this was some-thing else...

I felt my eyes go wide.

"Yes," he said, with a small nod. "I see you remember me now."

"Can't *remember* you," I said slowly. "Never met you before."

"No, of course not. But I did correspond with your partners and friends for a brief period. Back when they were hopeful of bringing me into the studio for a demonstration of my skills. Back before—"

The hands I held up now were open-palmed, and halting.

"We both know back before what."

"Do we?" One silver eyebrow ascended a millimeter. "I wonder."

"You were the one who got them killed."

"I did no such—"

"Not directly," I said with a sigh. "I don't blame you for their deaths or anything." I shook my head. "It was arguing about you with the network that got us sent out to Missouri that night."

"I know," he said with a small nod. "And I should probably have approached you years ago. But the truth was—"

"Wait," I said. "How did you *find* me? I'm not exactly in the book."

"I'm terribly sorry," Mr. Xerxes said with a small glint in his eye. "I thought you understood who I am."

"You're telling me your psychic powers helped you track me down?"

"No," he said gently. "I'm telling you that what you call my 'psychic powers' led me straight across the country to the exact spot where you chose to take your rest this morning."

That left me with a bunch of questions, but the old habits died harder than I thought.

"If you don't call them psychic powers, what do you call them?"

"They are simply skills, no more." His tone was so gentle and modest, he might have been talking about having fine handwriting. "Most people ignore them. I have made it the habit of a lifetime to perfect them."

"And you expect me to believe that?"

"Oh, dear." His turn to sigh. "I'd thought that, as you were once a paranormal investigator, you might be more amenable to possibilities beyond the normal. Especially given your personal experiences."

"Let's leave my personal experiences out of this."

"I'm afraid that your personal experiences are of paramount

importance," he said, with a slow shaking of his head. "I wish it were otherwise, Mr. Robertson. Truly I do."

"That's it," I said. "I'm out of here."

I didn't make it two steps back toward my jogging path before he stopped me with his next words.

"A test then? Will that suffice?"

And here I thought I'd left my "investigator" habits behind me entirely.

"What kind of test?" I narrowed my eyes in suspicion. "I'm not going anywhere private with you."

"Of course not," he said, and I have to admit he sounded as though the idea had never occurred to him. "You clearly do not believe I can do what I say, and you clearly to not wish to talk with me."

He smiled. Not a big, wide smile, but a small, confident smile.

"However," he said, "if you will do me only a single favor, I shall prove to you beyond a shadow of a doubt that I possess the skills I claim. And once I have done so—"

"Yeah, right." I snorted.

"Once I have done so, then you will do me the courtesy of hearing me out."

"Assuming I agree to this," I said slowly, "what kind of test?"

"Simple. Go out for lunch today. Pick any restaurant you want."

"In town?"

"Anywhere within, let's say, an hour's drive of here. Does that sound reasonable?"

I nodded.

"Excellent," he said with a bigger smile. "Then when you walk in the door, look for me. If I am already seated at a table, you must join me for lunch and hear me out. If I am not present, you will never hear from me again. You have my word as a gentleman."

That last sentence should have made me laugh out loud. I mean a good, solid guffaw. But something about this guy made me believe he did take his word that seriously.

"All right," I said, shaking my head. "I'll go out for lunch today.

And if you're already in that restaurant, waiting for me, I'll not only hear you out. I'll buy your lunch."

"On that part, Mr. Robertson, I must ask you to demur."

Took me a moment to understand what he was saying on that one. He didn't want me to buy his lunch? Before I could say anything, he continued, in a soft voice.

"I'm afraid your life is about to become difficult, Mr. Robertson. I will aid you if I can, but you must at least let me buy you lunch."

The sincerity in those gray eyes scared me more than sunset.

I just gave him a quick nod and went back to my jogging.

Finishing my morning run helped. Nothing like a fresh batch of endorphins under a clear blue sky to convince me that the boogeyman wasn't real.

The sun was shining. The only people I met were friendly. Overall, with the one glaring omission, it had been a good morning so far.

It was that omission I needed to think about.

I got back home before nine. Plenty of time to shower and shave, and still enjoy a light breakfast of fruit and hardboiled eggs over my morning paper, without risking ruining my lunch.

In fact, as the hours ticked past, I started to wonder about lunch. And more importantly, about this Mr. Xerxes.

How did this guy track me down?

I busted out my laptop for a little old fashioned research at the table in my small kitchen nook.

Doing research here and now made me nostalgic and wistful. I hadn't done anything like this since before that night in Missouri.

Hadn't wanted to. Hadn't even thought about it.

As I started digging around online, I couldn't help but feel their ghosts around me now.

Page leaning over my shoulder the way she used to when she spotted a key phrase or a link she wanted me to click on.

Todd pacing back and forth, tossing out ideas. Reading off some of his own research, from his phone. Peripheral stuff, intended to lead us to deeper findings.

Tangi, over at the gas stove or maybe the granite counter. Listening, always listening. Whether he was cooking or making coffee or what. Tangi, he hated being at the computer, except to edit. Hated sitting still unless it was for the video work he loved.

So during the research phase of our show, he was always doing something. If it wasn't food, he'd be shuffling a deck of cards, or twiddling a stick. Anything to give him something else to do while we did our research.

Page used to say he should take up knitting.

But Tangi was always listening. Quick to point out anything he thought would look good on camera. Any kind of setting that would rock for us, any person's image he thought the camera would love.

Page and Todd, they were all about the paranormal. Tangi, he was all about the shot. The scene. The cut. The episode.

Tangi saved us countless hours. He had an instinctive sense of running time. How long a segment would actually need, and when we looked like we might come up short.

I had to pause and walk away from the computer three times that morning. Just … air too thick with ghosts.

Still, I managed to dig around enough to realize that the only people calling Mr. Xerxes a fraud had never seen him in action.

Mind you, not many people had seen him at all. He'd done a couple of television shows in the 70s and 80s, but as the 90s came along, he retreated from the spotlight.

Probably could have had plenty of internet fame, if he'd let himself, but it seemed that the last time he contacted anyone about a public appearance, it had been Todd and Page.

Eight years ago.

After they … after that night in Missouri, Mr. Xerxes faded from the public eye entirely.

There was even a rumor that he'd died.

That was something I had to think about for a few minutes. Sent me back scouting around for any pictures I could find of anyone named Edmund Xerxes.

Not a common name. But since he'd been out of the public eye so long, all the pictures were at least twenty or twenty-five years old.

They could have been him. The old pictures had the bone structure. Had the eye color.

Believable.

But that didn't mean he was a psychic.

Yeah, he hadn't been debunked, but no one had tried since the 80s. Lots of progress on that front since then. And most of what passed for "proof" was really anecdotal.

Nothing Page or Todd would have taken as gospel. That was part of the reason they wanted to get him into the studio themselves.

So, if he wasn't a psychic, he might have been a detective. Wouldn't be hard to track me down by my SSN, driver's license. From there, all it would have taken was basic surveillance skills.

He could have been out there in the park every day this month, just waiting for me to show up. No reason anyone would notice him. Hell, *I* didn't have a reason to notice him. Not until he drew my attention.

No, it might have sounded like psychic powers, but a good working knowledge of street-level psychology and some solid detective work could look just like a psychic.

So. What did it mean to me either way?

I had promised to go out to lunch today. No reason I had to keep that promise. Not like I owed him anything.

The moment I thought that, I felt a wave of cold.

I was still sitting in my nice, sunny kitchen. With its natural wood warmth. On one of the hotter days of the year, when I didn't have the AC on.

And yet, a wave of cold washed over me.

"Page?" I muttered.

Couldn't help myself. I mean, yeah I'd been talking about ghosts earlier, while I did research. But that was just a turn of phrase. I was talking about memories. Not anything spiritual or paranormal.

But a wave of cold? That was the kind of thing that Page and Todd always insisted was the real sign of a haunting.

And if Page or Todd were in the room with me now, they'd be mad as hell if I talked about skipping a chance to prove or debunk a psychic.

And Tangi, he'd be mad at me for talking about breaking my word. Wasn't like me, and that was something Tangi liked about me.

"Guys?" I said, looking around the kitchen. I didn't feel cold now, but I couldn't help checking anyway. Wasn't like I had one of Page's detectors with me. "If any of you are here, could you give me a sign?"

I looked around. Made myself so still I couldn't hear anything but my own heartbeat. I wasn't even breathing.

Then I heard something — a car started, across the street. Followed a moment later by a lawnmower starting up down the block.

I chuckled at myself, and started breathing again.

There were no signs. There were no ghosts. There were no psychics.

But fine. I'd go out for lunch today. Just because my old partners would want me to.

But I wasn't going to make this easy on the old crackpot.

IN LIVING THE WAY I HAD FOR SO LONG, BACK WHEN I WAS STILL PART OF *Seekers*, I'd long since developed the habit of finding all the mom and pop joints in an area.

That was great for the show, because mom and pop places had *atmosphere*. They had friendly people who wanted to talk, especially about anything local and interesting.

Oh, they weren't all like that, but enough of them were that, professionally, it was well worth my time to seek them out.

On a more personal note, we did so much traveling that I was going to be damned before I'd eat at the same old place every day of the freaking week.

No, the mom and pop places tended to have better food, and more local varieties than I could have found at any of the chain restaurants.

So when I moved to Rancho Verde, I got to know all the little mom and pop places. Not just in Rancho Verde, but all over the greater Sacramento area.

That meant I had plenty of places to choose from.

The question was which one to pick.

If this Mr. Xerxes was playing a game with me, he'd expect me to make it hard for him. He'd set a limit of a one-hour drive, and I assumed he meant at legal speeds. That meant within about sixty-five miles.

Plenty of options, even at the periphery.

And I was sure he'd check the periphery first.

Maybe he'd been surveilling me for weeks. Maybe he'd figured out all my favorite places. No doubt he'd cross those off the list right away, as too obvious. Anyone I knew from work might have picked one of those as someplace I'd go to lunch.

So I did the best I could.

I went entirely against type.

I picked a chain restaurant I'd never go to. Not fast food, that was too easy. No, it was well known that I liked all different varieties of food, so I picked the most obvious, over-the-top Americana sit-down restaurant I could.

Banana Splits.

Can't miss Banana Splits. That's even their freaking slogan. They're everywhere. Every city. Seemingly every freeway exit on the long-haul drives. I would have sworn that I could have been air-dropped anywhere in the continental United States, and wouldn't have had more than a five mile walk to a Banana Splits.

Boring, typical American diner food, with a heavy focus on break-fasts and pies. Their servers all wore at least two dozen "cute" pins each.

Ways to express themselves, or something. Maybe just a

marketing thing, since each Banana Splits also sold at least a dozen varieties of buttons.

On my own, I'd never be caught dead in a Banana Splits.

Even better, a quick 'net search told me there were a dozen within an hour's drive of me.

I printed their addresses. Cut them out. Mixed them up. Shuffled them, face down.

Then I wrote numbers on their backs. One number each.

I looked up a random number generator on a website.

I pulled random numbers between one and twelve until one number came up twice.

That number was three.

So I picked Banana Splits number three. Four miles from where I was sitting, down I5.

I stood up, the address in my hand, and smiled.

All right, Mr. Xerxes. Let's see your detective and psychology skills help you guess this one.

Two glass doors to pass through before I was inside Banana Splits proper. Like it needed an airlock between the restaurant and reality.

An airlock where they could give away stacks of free local papers and sell gumballs from a big, glass spiral machine. They even had a little community board, tacked up against a glass sidewall, advertising guitar lessons and garage sales.

A quick glance, then I was through the second set of glass doors and inside the restaurant I'd avoided most of my adult life.

Two things hit me immediately.

The first was a blast of refrigerated air that immediately made me regret wearing nothing more than cargo shorts and a lightweight Giants tee shirt, to go with my sandals.

Goosebumps leapt to my defense, all across my skin.

The other thing that hit me was the smell of pastry.

Donuts. I would have sworn I smelled donuts.

Didn't make any sense to me. I mean, I could smell plenty of bacon. That was to be expected. And grease, of course. Places like this lived and died by their grease.

But donuts?

That was strange.

Only to me though. My lack of prior patronage had apparently done nothing to diminish the average American's love of this restaurant chain. With dozens of other establishments nearby, Banana Splits was still so full the air was bursting with a cacophony of chatter and clatter.

Wait staff whisked by, carrying more or carrying away the leavings. Buttons all over their clothes. Some just on their signature black-and-yellow vests. Others had buttons on their polo shirts, buttons on their khaki slacks. One even had buttons on his shoelaces.

Here in the entryway, two benches overflowed with families waiting for tables to free up.

I stepped between them across the thin carpet to the harried teenage girl at the podium, with her frizzy hair and frazzled eyes.

"Hi," I said. "Table for one?"

"Name?" she asked, not even looking at me. Just grabbed up a well-chewed Bic and prepared to add my name to the end of a long list scrawled on her yellow tablet.

"His name is Selwyn Robertson," Mr. Xerxes said, voice carrying from somewhere out of eyeshot. "But you don't need to write his name down, dear. He's the guest I've been waiting for."

I turned right, and there he was. Same blue suit. Same neutral-pleased expression. Except this time he had something of a self-satisfied glint to his gray eyes.

But what the hell. He'd earned it.

"All right," I said, extending my hand. "I'm impressed."

"Thank you," he said, shaking my hand. His grip was surprisingly strong, considering his skin felt so smooth I doubted he'd ever done a real day's work. "Our table is this way."

He led me to a booth back along the wall.

A booth in what appeared to be a closed section of the restaurant.

"Umm..." I started, but he held up a hand to forestall my question.

"A favor from the manager. I helped him find his lost dog this morning. When I mentioned that I would appreciate privacy, he couldn't help me fast enough."

"How long have you been here?"

"Well," he said, easing himself down onto the padded vinyl seat with no small measure of grace, "I couldn't be certain what time you would arrive. And our agreement required me to already be seated. So I'm afraid I've been here for some time now."

That dropped my jaw faster than I dropped myself into my seat. The padded bench farted out air beneath me.

"How?" I asked. "I didn't know myself where I'd be until maybe ten minutes ago. Fifteen at the outside."

"That doesn't matter," he said with a small shake of his head. "*When* you decided had no bearing on *what* you'd decide."

"But I selected it randomly."

"Is anything truly random?"

"Wait," I said, holding up both hands. This was going too quickly for me. "Wait. Are you saying there's no such thing as free will? That where I was going to be for *lunch* was ... what ... *foretold*?"

"Well," he said through a sigh, "if you want to be *technical*, it was foretold. Because *I* foretold it about two hours ago."

An explosive response started in my gut, but didn't reach my mouth, because Mr. Xerxes held up a restraining hand. Something about the gesture eased all the power out of my chosen swear word. All that came out was a weak puff of air.

"However," he said, before I could ask about what he might have just done to me, "please don't mistake my little prediction as an indication that you lack free will. Why people always leap to that conclusion is quite beyond me."

"But—"

"It is as though they believe the universe must be entirely stochastic, with every element, even our own thoughts and feelings subject to nothing more than the whims of whatever moment unfurls them, or that everything from the time they take their first breath to the timing of their daily restroom breaks must be part of some great divine plan."

He shook his head.

"It's really quite maddening in its oversimplification."

"May I speak?" I asked.

"Oh, yes, of course," he said, looking chagrined. "Do forgive me, please. It's rather a touchy subject for me, you must understand."

"I'm not sure I'm following you. If where I was going to go to lunch today was already set. If it was something that could be predicted. How then, can you claim that I made a choice of my own free will? How can it be that I had no choice other than to be *here*?"

"Oh, and I suppose I'm infallible, am I?"

That made me blink.

"Yes," he said, "I predicted where you would be. But the accuracy of my prediction depended upon a number of factors. Factors I have trained my entire life to minimize, true, but still, factors that could have come into play and caused me to err."

"Factors such as what?" The question came out by reflex. I wasn't sure I wanted to know, but I'd come this far.

"Oh, my own ability to achieve a properly neutral state, free of arrogance or assumption. My ability to gain a sense of you. My facility with my chosen tool for divination. Among others."

"You can be good with a crystal ball?"

"If I were a crystal gazer," Mr. Xerxes said with a sardonic raised eyebrow, "then I rather assume I would practice at it until I gained a degree of proficiency that made my attempts useful. Otherwise, what would be the point?"

"So you saw me sitting here? In a crystal ball?"

"Of course not," he said. "I've never been able to see more than my own reflection in a crystal ball. I am skilled. I am not omniscient."

We were interrupted by our server then. A puzzled looking boy not quite old enough to shave, who clearly wasn't sure why we were in this section, but had been told not to question it.

Or maybe he was wondering if he should have recognized us. This close to the state capital, anyone as old and white as Mr. Xerxes might just be a politician.

And I probably looked like a reporter, the way I was peppering Mr. Xerxes with questions.

Our little discussion ground to a halt then, so we could place our order. I had coffee, scrambled eggs, a bowl of fruit, and — damn that infectious smell — a set of Banana Splits' signature donut waffles.

Mr. Xerxes joined me for the coffee, but his lunch was much simpler than mine. Three hardboiled eggs. Two slices of dry wheat toast. A single half of cantaloupe.

I was downright shocked that they had that last thing. Hadn't seen it on the menu. But the kid wrote it all down as though he took that order all the time.

Then he was gone, and I looked back at Mr. Xerxes, brimming with questions.

I couldn't believe I was doing this.

Not just that I was having lunch in a Banana Splits. Not even that I'd just ordered donut waffles.

I couldn't believe I was seriously interviewing a psychic. After eight years away from any kind of paranormal stuff.

This had to be a mistake. This had to be a terrible, terrible mistake.

But I'd promised that if Mr. Xerxes met me here, I'd hear him out. So I couldn't do the natural thing and go running out of this restaurant, screaming my way back into the little hole I'd been hiding in for the last three years.

I looked across the table at him. He still sat with perfect, textbook posture, looking like an ad for a high class retirement community.

His eyes seemed sad, but patient. As though he could wait all day to hear what I had to say next.

But there were so many questions, I wasn't sure what I wanted to say. What I wanted to know.

Check that. I didn't really want to know any of it. But I couldn't help myself. Maybe I owed it to Todd, Page and Tangi. Maybe I owed it to myself.

Or maybe those old reflexes just died that hard.

"Go ahead," he said with an encouraging nod. "Ask. Ask anything you want. The better you understand who I am and what I do, the better my chances of persuading you to listen to what I have to say."

"Maybe we should just—"

"No," he said, slowly shaking his head. "Please. Ask. It's better this way."

"Fine." I drew a deep breath. Let it out slowly. "If you didn't use a crystal ball, how did you find me?"

"With the pendulum," he said. He reached into the pocket in his suit jacket's liner, and pulled out a small, pointed piece of polished wood, hanging at the end of a silver chain.

"The silver is something of an indulgence, I fear," he admitted. "Cord would do, but I felt I deserved to treat myself, in that regard. After all, I had harvested, shaped, and lacquered the teak myself."

I pointed at the dangling bit of wood. "That led you to me?"

"The process is called—"

"Dowsing," I said, nodding. "I know. Most use two pieces of bent metal to do it, but some use a pendulum."

"Precisely," he said with a pleased smile. "Finding your location for lunch was a simple matter of choosing maps and applying the skills of my trade."

"Is it?"

"I'm sorry?"

"Is it your trade? Do you make your living dowsing?"

"Well," — a small flush lit his cheeks — "while I do not ply my skills for payment, I do rather make my way through life with them."

"Gambling or stock market?"

"Rather."

I chuckled. Both then. And probably a couple of other things besides. But then, it had been a pretty personal question.

"All right," I said. "Page and Todd said you did remote viewing. What does a pendulum have to do with remote viewing?"

"Little. And everything." He made a fifty-fifty motion with his hand. "The skill sets are related in the disciplines of my training. Which I use depends on which strikes me as the better route to my destination. Intuition is a large part of what I do."

"So why choose the pendulum to find my lunch spot?"

"For me — and I do not speak for every remote viewer now, only myself — I find remote viewing into the present and past far easier than into the future. The question of where you would take your lunch was, for me, more easily determined with a map and a pendulum than in trying to cast my mind into what would yet be."

"And if I broke my promise? If I hadn't gone out for lunch?"

Mr. Xerxes smiled. "Then the pendulum would have led me to your home, and I would have knocked on your door."

I must have looked doubtful, because he reached into his suit pocket again.

"Shall I seek your address right now?" he asked. "I have my map and pendulum. If it will help you to understand—"

"There's no need for that," I said, raising my cup of coffee like a stop sign.

"As you like," Mr. Xerxes said, and folded his hands on the Formica table.

"Fine," I said. "You really are a psychic, and you really did track me down with your psychic pow... With your skills. Is that what you wanted to hear?"

"Normally, it would not matter to me one way or the other what you believe."

He waited then, as our coffee was brought and our water glasses were refilled. Hadn't even realized I'd drunk any, but my glass was empty.

Now that I thought about it, I could feel the chill in my mouth, the slightly metallic taste of public tap water on my tongue.

Apparently I'd been more focused on all this than I'd thought.

Once the server was going, Mr. Xerxes continued.

"I needed you to believe me in this case, I'm afraid, because you need to understand that I have the skills to know the things I know. You must believe that, or you might not believe what I have to tell you."

"What?" I said, and it came out loud enough I was glad the tables near us were empty. I didn't bother keeping my voice down though. "What is so damned important that you had to track me down on my day off and play psychic with me?"

Mr. Xerxes drew a breath. Slowly. Maybe he needed to ignore something in what I'd just said, or maybe he was girding himself for what he said next.

"Mr. Robertson," he said, "that vampire was real. And it's looking for you."

For a moment, I couldn't believe what I'd just heard.

For a moment, I sat, muscles locked in place. Heart pounding.

My jaw clenched as I counted to ten.

Then again.

Then a third time.

I tried to distract myself. To lose myself in the sounds of the diner. The clatter of dishes. The happy, casual laughter of children nearby. The lament of teenagers who'd rather be anywhere else on a Saturday than out to a meal with their families.

The scents of grease and donuts and bacon filled my nose with every breath.

But no matter what I heard or smelled, I couldn't see anything except Mr. Xerxes. Those sad gray eyes. That neutral set to his face and lips. That razor perfect posture. Hands folded on the Formica table, between his cup of coffee and his glass of water.

And Mr. Xerxes, he didn't say anything more for a moment. He just looked back at me. Neutral.

That was some trick, in itself.

If he'd given me any kind of wrong stare, I'd probably have hit him. If he'd challenged me, or accused me, or just been *watching* for a response.

Anything like that.

But no, he sat there, even more neutral than most of my therapists had managed, while I absorbed what he just told me.

But just because this guy was a psychic, didn't mean he had the right to bring back my fucking delusion. No matter what he thought he saw. No matter what he thought he knew.

I drew a long, slow breath through my nose. Deep enough to fill my whole chest, and my chest took some filling.

I blew that breath back out, just as slow.

And Mr. Xerxes said nothing.

Finally, I broke the silence between us.

"How dare you?"

"Mr. Robertson, I assure—"

"How fucking *dare* you?"

"Mr. Robertson—"

"You come in here playing psychic, and you try to bring back the *delusion* that kept me in a fucking *nuthouse* for *five years*?"

"Oh, I—"

"My parents were footing the bill for that, you know. They never complained, but I know it wasn't cheap."

Mr. Xerxes stopped trying to talk then. Just listened.

"They even came to visit me. Regularly. But somewhere along the line, they lost hope. Some part of me died in their eyes. I saw it happen. And there was nothing I could do about it."

I stared deep into Mr. Xerxes' sad gray eyes. Willed this bastard to understand what I'd gone through. What he was trying to bring back.

"Even after I got out. Released," I said, raising one finger. "Not escaped. Certificate of sanity and all. My own parents figured I was there for life. But I. Got. Out."

With those last three words I jabbed the table with my finger hard enough to rattle our dishes and flatware.

I let those words hang for a moment, before spitting what I said next right in his face.

"And *still*, they look at me and see something broken."

I threw all the challenge at him I could. Nothing in Mr. Xerxes eyes, though, but sad sympathy. Or maybe empathy. I never did quite get the difference.

It was too much. The way my heart was pounding. The way I'd started sweating. My skin all fever-hot. The rush of my own blood past my ears. All that contrasted with whatever I saw in those eyes of his.

Just ... too much.

I had to look away from him. All but mumbled my next words.

"And I can't say they're wrong."

My mouth dried up on me. I had to drink down half my tinny ice water before I could continue.

And Mr. Xerxes, he was still letting me talk.

"It's been eight *fucking years* since my friends died. And I still don't know what really happened to them. Because when I think back, all I remember is a *lie*, brought on by stress, exhaustion, and physical and emotional trauma."

I glared at Mr. Xerxes. Tried to goad him. Dared him to interrupt me. Contradict me. Anything.

He still sat there. Listening, but otherwise impassive.

I'm not even sure he blinked.

So I kept talking.

"I still can't go out after dark. Did your pendulum tell you that? Did it tell you I'm still fucked up enough that I may never live a normal life? That I still haven't..."

More water. Then coffee.

I had to slam my fist on the table before I could continue. When I did, all the anger was out of my voice. There was no room for anything now but pure sadness.

"I still haven't been able to say a proper goodbye to my three best friends."

I shook my head. Took another deep breath. Slapped a more combative tone back into place.

"And now you come here with your silk suits in ninety degree weather, and you tell me that your goddamn *pendulum* has told you I really squared off with a vampire. And somehow survived, while all my friends got killed."

I shook my head again, but this time in disgust.

"Tell the truth now. You read about me in one of those wacko forums. I know the rumors flew wild as soon as I got put into the hospital. And I don't even mean the nuthouse. Just the regular hospital. Showing up as I did, damn near out of blood, throat ripped open and raving about vampires. No way that was kept out of the news or off the internet."

I ran out of steam for a moment, but Mr. Xerxes, if nothing else, was a good listener. He could tell I wasn't finished, and he was willing to wait.

"Hell," I said finally, just loud enough to hear myself over the background of loud, if distant, conversation and the clatter of dishes and flatware. "Even I've seen a few of the videos people keep posting and reposting, faster than cease-and-desist orders can stop them." I shook my head. "Network's probably behind it. Drumming up interest in syndication of the old replays. At least the bastards still pay residuals."

I ran out of steam then. Finished my coffee for something to do. Looked around for my lunch, but it wasn't here yet.

I was just about ready to call for our server, when Mr. Xerxes finally spoke.

"The young lad will be along in a few minutes," he said, his voice calm. Not a hint of challenge. "Our food isn't ready yet. The kitchen staff is backed up. It seems that some of our fellow diners have been sending their food back over niggling complaints, and slowing the process for everyone else."

I looked back at Mr. Xerxes. His eyes were calm, if still a little sad. His skin showed no signs of stress, even though I'd been going at him for some time now.

"I can assure you, if it helps," he continued, "that our food will arrive hot. The manager has promised that to no fewer than three other customers, and so far he has not been wrong."

That actually reached past my fog of anger, sadness and recriminations.

How could he know all that?

"Remote viewing?" I asked.

He nodded. "I was still listening to you, of course. Test me if you wish. But your hunger is most apparent. I could tell you would need food soon, so I checked. If it would help, I have a packet of crackers in my pocket."

"No thanks," I said, narrowing my eyes as I heard my stomach rumble hard at the thought of crackers.

If my stomach had complained before then, I hadn't noticed. But I was starting to believe Mr. Xerxes had.

The man was observant. I had to give him that.

"Please," Mr. Xerxes said, with apparently perfect sincerity, "do forgive me, Mr. Robertson. I in no way wish to cause you trauma. Indeed, I wish to *save* you trauma."

"Then—"

"Forgive me," he said firmly, "but you did promise to hear me out. And I'm afraid I must insist that you do. Whether you believe me or not, I cannot help. But I must do everything I can, nevertheless."

"Why?" I asked, and even I could hear the urgency in my voice. "Why do you need to help me? Why do you..." I shook my head. "Just ... why?"

"Mr. Robertson," he said, "my skills are not a mere matter of training, no matter what impression I give. Training alone is simply insufficient, for most people, to develop enough proficiency with ... extranormal skills, to find them worth investing larger amounts of time in."

He tilted his head as he considered his words. "It is a matter of one's calling. If one is called to work with one's extranormal skills, then the proper instructors and techniques will be drawn to that individual. However, there is a price for such development."

"Price?"

Mr. Xerxes answer was interrupted by the arrival of our food, and refills for our drinks.

My donut waffles were piping hot.

I ate hungrily while Mr. Xerxes continued.

"Sometimes the price is simple. A person is drawn to me, whether they know of my skills or not, that I might help them. One of the reasons I do not accept payment, you see. The people who come to me for help, they are often at their wits end. To profit from a time of such need would be unseemly."

He sipped his coffee, then buttered his toast, nibbling at it as he continued.

"And then there are times when I see things I have no wish to see. Things I was not attempting to see. Would never wish to know. And yet I must see these things. I must know. And it is clear to me that, when I see these unwanted things, I must take action. I must help those people as I can."

I couldn't help interrupting him.

"And I suppose you saw that night, did you?"

Mr. Xerxes got a faraway look in his eye. Enough so that I almost wondered if he *was* far away in that moment, which meant he definitely had me believing in his psychic powers. Skills. Whatever.

"I was attempting to remote view the remains of an old riverboat, sunk in the Mississippi about a hundred and fifty years ago. The stories said that a fortune in gold — both United States gold and a small amount of stamped, Confederate gold coins — had sunk with it, never to be recovered. The pendulum had brought me to the right area, but—"

"Wait," I said. "The Confederacy used paper money. They didn't mint gold."

"They did. Not much, on the grand scale of stamped coins, but that only adds to the value of the coins they did mint."

My next attempted question was lost in a mouthful of egg, waffle, and maple syrup. I had to swallow some coffee before I could repeat it.

"If the pendulum got you to the right spot, why remote view?"

"Through the pendulum I found the site of the sunken riverboat. But I needed to see the wreckage, before hiring an expedition. I had to know that I would find something that would at least pay my costs."

"And what does this have to do with me?"

"That riverboat is what I was attempting to scry when I saw something else. Something I neither attempted to see, nor wished to witness, but nevertheless was forced to watch."

Mr. Xerxes got a haunted look in his eyes then. It was a look I knew well. I'd seen it in the mirror for the last eight years.

Seeing it on his face now was like stepping outside into a cold, sudden rain.

I stopped eating. Nodded to him.

"Tell me," I said softly.

"You know what I saw," he said, just as softly. "I saw you and your friends, pull up next to an all-but-forgotten cemetery. I saw you stalking through the woods. I saw you standing over a patch of dead grass at the back of that cemetery. I saw you interrupted by a vampire, and I saw the vampire's attack."

Thinking back to that moment in the restaurant, I'm amazed I didn't deny what he'd just said. I'd been denying it for so long, it was reflex more often than it wasn't.

But maybe it was something in the old man's eyes. Or maybe it was the way he'd convinced me about his skills. Or maybe ... maybe I just wanted to believe that after all these years, I could get an answer to the two questions that had burned at me.

"What happened to Page and Tangi?" I asked, leaning forward on the table so fast I put my elbow in my maple syrup.

"I believe the vampire took them along. I have tried to look for them since, but I haven't been able to acquire a sufficient connection to them to—"

"But what do you mean the vampire took them? Where? Where did they go?"

"I don't know," he said, shaking his head slowly. "I'm sorry. I wish I could answer that. But a seeing like this, I had no control over it. I saw you more than I saw anything else."

"But—"

"After the vampire threw Todd Jeffries at you, he hefted Tangi Maaka and threw him down the road. Farther that you would have believed a man like Tangi could be thrown. Page Carmichael screamed at the sight."

"And Page?"

"Page ... locked eyes with him. Froze in place. Then the vampire came to you. Looked down at you and said—"

"I remember," I said. To this day I can still hear his voice. "Wooden bullets? Ultraviolet light? How can you study so much and learn so little?"

Mr. Xerxes nodded. Then asked softly. "Do you remember what came next?"

I shook my head.

"He ... feasted on you."

"But Page. Tangi."

Mr. Xerxes shook his head. "I don't know. I only saw him feast on you and Todd Jeffries."

"What stopped him? Why didn't he finish me?"

"I don't know. The image faded with your consciousness."

"But where did he take Tangi and Page? If the cemetery was his home, why weren't they found there? Where could they have gone? Dawn was only minutes away."

"I don't know," he said, hanging his head forward and sounding sadder than I'd heard him yet. "I'm sorry. I wish I had the answers to all your questions, but I don't. I do not jest when I say I'm not infallible. I tried. I tried harder than you would believe to find out what happened that night. Where your friends were taken. Why you were left alive. What became of the vampire. Only to that last question have I been able to find anything like an answer."

I wanted to scream and yell at the unfairness of it all. How I could come so close to so many answers, only to have those answers ripped away again.

But I'd forgotten something. I'd gotten so caught up in our conversation, that I'd forgotten what Mr. Xerxes said in the first place.

I forgot … until he reminded me.

"The vampire," he said, "I have found again. And it is looking for you."

I had to blink at him. That didn't compute. Something about the idea of the vampire hunting for me after all these years clashed in my mind.

Then I figured out why.

"Oh fuck this," I said, shaking my head long and slow. "You actually had me going, you son of a bitch. You spin a good yarn, I'll grant you, and I don't know how you—"

"Mr. Robertson, don't do this."

"No," I said, getting louder. "Don't *you* do this. There's no such things as vampires. I don't know what psych games you played to get me here, or beat me here, or whatever. Hell, maybe you do have some psychic powers. But what happened to me that night, that wasn't a vampire."

"It was, Mr. Robertson." His voice was as calm and confident as ever, despite the fact that he was facing two-hundred-fifty pounds of angering muscle.

"Fifteen psychiatrists and four hypnotherapists disagree with you."

"Most of the world disagrees with me about a great many things. That does not mean I am always wrong. And I am right about this."

I got up. "I heard you out. Right? You agree I heard you out?"

"If you leave now, you miss the entire purpose of my coming here," Mr. Xerxes said through a long sigh. "But yes. I agree you have heard me out. If you're so very certain you wish to bury your head in the sand, then leave."

I turned away.

"Go die like your friends," he said. "I cannot help you if you will not let me."

I spun around and grabbed him by both lapels so fast he didn't have time to react.

Or maybe he was still just that calm.

Either way, I leaned in closer.

"Listen, asshole," I said. "I don't know what your game is. What you really want here. But you're through talking about my friends. If I ever see or hear from you again, I'll break bones you can't afford to heal at your age."

"No," he said, and for the first time I heard something like fire in his voice. Saw something blaze in those gray eyes. "You listen. I understand what you've been through. I understand what it means to have the world beat you down. Claim you could never have experienced what you did."

"I'm warning you—"

"Page warned you," he said. "Demanded you all carry weapons. Because she saw the signs and knew what they meant. Was Page a fool?"

That got me to let go of his lapels. He didn't straighten them then though, he just held me with those burning eyes as he kept talking.

"Was Todd? Because he knew she was right. They both knew. Even if you and Tangi didn't believe. Even if you were humoring them. Disbelief gives you no protection from the things that stalk the night, no matter what people wish to say."

I dropped back into the other side of the booth and listened as he continued.

"I know you were committed against your will. I know that's the only reason you never went after the vampire. I know the doctors battered at your psyche for years, with all their tools. With drugs. With trances. With endless discussions, both one-on-one and in group settings. Used the beliefs of society against you. Used the social proof of those groups."

Mr. Xerxes slowly shook his head, never taking his eyes from mine.

"But truth, Mr. Robertson, is not a matter of social proof. You went looking for a vampire that night. And you found one."

"Page was a fool," I said, finally giving voice to something I held down for eight years. Even then, I hated myself for saying it. "And so was Todd."

"Mr. Robertson—"

"Hear me out," I said, raising a halting hand. I knew I sounded tired, and maybe the exhaustion in my voice was what made Mr. Xerxes listen to me then.

Because he nodded for me to continue.

"Let's just say for a second here, that you're right. That it wasn't some trick of exhaustion, blood loss and trauma. We really did find a ..." — I drew a long, fast breath and let it out — "what we went there to find. That it all happened just the way I remember."

Mr. Xerxes nodded, completely neutral and listening once more.

"If Page and Todd knew vampires were real," I said. "And I'm pretty damned sure they did. If they knew that, then they were fools to go after one. Because the way I remember it, there's no beating that thing."

"That's not entirely true, Mr. Robertson."

"Yes it is," I said, sliding to the end of the booth seat. "We hit it with everything we had, and it made jokes."

"Your friends' only error was their choice of weapons."

"The only *right* weapon," I said, standing up, "is staying the fuck away from it. And whether it was real or all in my head, that's all I intend to do."

But before I walked away I offered Mr. Xerxes my hand to shake.

"I get that you're trying to help," I said, as he shook my hand with a remarkably cool, dry grip. "In your own weird way. But if this thing is real. If this thing wants to kill me, it will. And there's not a damned thing I can do about it."

Mr. Xerxes offered me a business card.

"You are not the only survivor, Mr. Robertson. There are others. And these creatures are not omnipotent. They can be vanquished. Please. When you are ready, contact me."

I couldn't believe I was doing it, but I took his card before I left.

5

———————

The summer heat felt good on my skin.

I barely made it three steps down the concrete sidewalk outside the glass doors of Banana Splits before I stopped and just turned my closed eyes up to the afternoon sun.

Heat. Blessed heat. Dry. Pushing a hundred, yes. Already palpable all over the skin of my arms and legs, my neck and face, yes.

But it was *real*. Nothing to doubt there.

Mr. Xerxes, maybe he was real, maybe not. He sure played a good game, no doubts there. And I gave him full marks for observation. But that would be part of his trade, if he were a con man.

Even that bit with the manager and the food. He might have been able to tune into other conversations while I was saying things he didn't intend to respond to anyway.

I had no way to know he'd been listening to me the whole time. Could've been an act.

As for the things he told me...

I blew it.

The one big thing I had to test him on. The one big thing he could have told me that I'd never told anyone else. That one thing, and I'd said it aloud. I'd let him lead me along the events of the evening right up to that point, and I'd said the words myself.

The words spoken by … the vampire? My delusion?

Whatever. If Mr. Xerxes had really watched that moment happen, I should have made *him* say those fucking words. Then I would have *known* he was on the level.

Proof positive.

But no. I did the same thing as every mark since time immemorial. I played along, and tipped too much information when I got emotionally involved.

And I was still emotionally involved right now.

My guts felt all knotted up, and I didn't think it was just those donut waffles.

Though, admittedly, they were probably a factor. I didn't usually eat shit like that, and no doubt they would have weighed heavily in my stomach, even without the turmoil.

But my heart was still pounding. Too much for too long to be healthy. Made me want to do something physical, just to *do something* with all that blood flow.

Run all the way home, maybe. Only four miles. Yeah, in hundred-degree heat, if my skin wasn't lying to me. But that wasn't why I didn't do it.

I didn't do it because I knew once I got home I wasn't leaving until at least dawn tomorrow. And I didn't want to leave my car in a Banana Splits parking lot.

People around me. I could hear them. Feel them.

Families and couples coming in from the parking lot. Some of them probably staring at the weirdo with eyes closed and face turned to the sun.

None of them dumb enough to approach me right now.

I listened to them shuffle along. Half of them not even caring enough about their steps to lift their feet as they walked. They just dragged their feet across the ground as though walking properly was too much effort.

That thought made me open my eyes. Look.

Just people. A little heavy, maybe, but most people were these days. This group, though. Dressed sloppy. Walked sloppy. And now they were about to eat sloppy.

They had life. My friends were dead, and these sloppy people were alive.

And *this* was all they were doing with that life.

My friends died trying to prove something. Trying to show us that the world was bigger and weirder than we wanted to think it was. "Fill in the cracks left gaping by conventional science." That was how Todd and Page liked to say it.

And my friends were dead.

These people. These shufflers. They wouldn't care.

If they ever watched *Seekers*, they were doing it to watch the pretty people, Todd and Page. Or maybe to thrill for a few seconds at the thought that ghosts might just be real. That maybe the little encounter they'd had when they were kids, or on some lonely night, maybe that had been more than their imagination.

One thing I learned working on *Seekers*. Most people had a story. Some encounter that wasn't easily explained by science or conventional wisdom. Wasn't always a haunting, and some of them wouldn't talk about it with strangers.

But most people had a story.

I never used to believe them. Todd and Page did. Tangi too, sometimes. Me, I just thought it was overactive imaginations, and the result of watching too many late shows.

And our show seemed to back me up. All the places we went in three seasons of *Seekers*, we never found a scrap of hard proof of anything supernatural. Not as far as I was concerned.

Oh, we found little teases. Things Todd and Page got excited about. Got them talking about the "accumulation of data outside sigma." And then they'd get *really* technical.

But nothing solid.

Unless...

Unless we did.

Exactly once.

I thought about those stories. The ones we used to hear in interviews, as well as the ones we'd brush up against that made interviewees clam up. The roadside hitchhiking ghosts. The strange sounds and cold spots at friends' houses or parents' houses or grandparents' houses.

All those little sightings and encounters that made the shufflers wonder. Gave them little stories to tell, if they felt comfortable enough.

But the thing that always bugged me about those stories was this — if these shufflers really believed those stories they told, how could they live normal lives? If Jake Flake from Donner Lake believed he really saw the ghost of a boy who drowned three years before, how could that not change his life?

If he really saw a *ghost*, if he really had an *encounter with the supernatural*, how could that not change his worldview from the ground up?

How could it be just a story he told once in a while?

Simple. Everyone knows ghosts aren't real. Any more than vampires.

That night eight years ago, at a forgotten cemetery on a Missouri back road. Was that *my* story? My event that couldn't be explained by science and conventional wisdom?

By fifteen doctors and four hypnotherapists?

Or were my memories of that night just what those learned men and women insisted? Delusions, brought on by trauma, et cetera.

I thought about that, again, and I shuffled my feet across the huge Banana Splits parking lot. Scraped the bottoms of my sandals along the hot asphalt. My nose filling with the smells of summertime heat, and cars, and sweaty people.

I shuffled my feet, because I was starting to wonder if I was just another goddamn shuffler.

My friends were dead.

I was alive.

And what was I doing with that life?

I did drive home. Slow. Speed limit slow. Made sure I turned on my blinker at least twenty feet before I was legally supposed to. Made sure I stayed in the right-hand lane the whole four miles.

All because I figured shufflers were the most law-abiding of drivers. The sort of drivers who got honked at every day, but felt righteous in their legality. Maybe they flipped the bird at passing drivers. Or maybe they sat, untouched, in an aura of smugness.

I didn't do either. I stared at the road and hoped my reflexes would notice brake lights and stop lights.

The shufflers may have been my excuse to drive that way, but I wasn't thinking about them.

Because my thoughts were all on that question.

What was I doing with my life?

Five years of therapy, but could I call myself healthy?

For crying out loud, I couldn't leave my house unless the sun was shining.

I lived alone.

I worked, yes, but I took jobs I thought were safe. No real fulfillment to it. Just a way to keep a roof over my head and food in my mouth.

I ate well, yes, but that wasn't a choice. It was a habit. My parents had stressed a good diet, and when I'd played football, it had become a necessity. Every little edge I could find.

I still exercised. Ran. Lifted weights. A little cross-training. All stuff I could do alone. In my garage, if need be.

I had no social life. No friends, apart from "work friends." But they weren't real friends. I hadn't had any real friends since that night.

I hadn't done anything to meet people. To find a community I could call myself a part of. Not since that night.

I hadn't...

I'd been surviving. Yes. But I hadn't been living.

Todd was dead. Angry Todd, with his many flavors of yelling. But that was just his way. Todd, he had my back more times than I could count.

When I didn't even get drafted for the NFL, Todd was the one who picked the lock on my apartment door. Forced me to get out of bed. To shower. To realize life went on.

Todd could be a major asshole. But only because we all knew that wasn't who he really was.

Page. Brilliant Page, with her dozens of patents and her quick smile and wit. How many times had I gone through a break-up, only to have Page verbally rip the girl apart. Sometimes even when the girl was present.

Well, if the girl was present, then Page thought the girl *deserved* to get ripped to shreds. If the girl was absent, Page did it to make me feel better.

Didn't matter either way. Page, she was one of a kind.

And Tangi. Did anyone ever have a better friend than Tangi? How many misadventures had we gotten into over the years? How many messes had we gotten each other into and out of?

We never got arrested. But we used to joke that if I ever woke up in a jail cell, Tangi would be sitting right next to me, big smile on his face, saying, "Soon as we get out, we gotta do that again."

Tangi was my brother in all but blood.

The three best friends I could have asked for.

And all three of them were dead.

I was still alive.

They were dead. I was alive.

And what would they say if they saw how I was living?

With thoughts like those in my head, it's a wonder I made even that short drive without hitting anything.

I didn't even reach any conclusions. Just a revolving set of questions, through that short drive.

I would have sworn the drive was forty miles, not four, the way my mind went through so many doubts, so many recriminations. So many questions.

The whole way, it was like I could feel the ghosts of my three best friends, all watching me. All asking me the same question.

What was I doing with my life?

But I made that drive home in one piece. And I did find myself stopping in my own driveway, so I must have been okay behind the wheel. I didn't even get ticketed for impeding traffic.

I got out of the car, and looked at where I was living.

I rented half of a duplex. One story. Ranch style. Technically an apartment, but it might as well have been a house. Except for the shared wall.

Neatly mown lawn. Tiny little Japanese maples stationed at either end of the lawn like guards.

A driveway on each side, so we could each have garages. They only saw use as storage for my neighbors. A nice little Russian family. Parents in their twenties, but two kids already. Both in elementary school not two blocks away.

They invited me to their monthly parties, without fail. But their parties were evening parties, so I always begged off. Listened as the hour grew later, and the vodka began to flow. Listened as my neighbors and their friends sang Russian folk songs late into the night.

They were living.

What was I doing?

My own garage didn't see much use as storage. I just didn't own enough for that. It was where I kept my workout equipment. My all-in-one weight machine. My treadmill. My kettlebell. Usual kind of stuff.

The one concession to comfort? I'd laid down a carpet. Once shaggy, maybe, but I'd gotten it secondhand at a thrift store. Now it was little more than a dark green pad with a little texture, if I walked on it in bare feet. Which I never did.

I spurned the garage for now. Walked in my front door, grabbing a handful of local circulars from my mailbox en route. No personal mail. Not for me.

My living room. A fifty-inch flat screen television. A high-end stereo — my professional ears could stand nothing less than a stereo that cost as much as my car — and a recliner. A single, fluorescent lamp, standing on one side of the recliner. A little oak end table on the other side.

No other chairs. Nothing on the walls.

Was this living?

The carpet was good for a rental. Dark blue, and thick. Did I ever wiggle my toes in it? Enjoy it?

No.

I wandered into the kitchen. Linoleum floor. Simple furnishings. Granite counter. A stove and oven I never used. A little griller that cooked two-thirds of what I ate. A microwave that cooked the rest of it. A high-end coffee maker, programmable, with temperature control and a grinder.

Just like with sound, I didn't like cheap coffee.

No.

I always told myself I didn't like cheap coffee.

I never *used* to like cheap coffee.

But I'd drunk three cups of coffee at Banana Splits. Did I even taste it?

Nothing else on the counter. Not even a blender.

I opened my silverware drawer. Enough flatware for four people to eat at the same time. In other words, for me to eat four meals.

I closed the drawer. Opened the cabinets.

No boxes of staples. A bunch of canned soups and foods, in case of emergency. Along with cases of water, for the same reason.

I didn't even know what emergency I was preparing for. I wasn't all that near any of California's major fault lines.

Four plates. Four bowls. Four glasses.

Most of my cabinet space: empty.

Was this living?

I wandered through my apartment that way. Looked in the second bedroom, where I'd set up my home studio. Where I hadn't recorded anything personal since I'd set it up.

My bathrooms, with barely enough supplies for me. If I ever did have an overnight guest, we'd have to share a towel.

Was this living?

I SPENT THE AFTERNOON THAT WAY. JUST LOOKING AT MY EXCUSE FOR A life. Feeling the ghosts of my friends watching me. I almost want to say judging me, but that would have been a lie.

Those three, they never judged me.

Any judgment I felt, that was coming from the inside.

I sat in my recliner and drank water and stewed about the day. About my meeting with Mr. Xerxes. About that night so long ago. About what my life had become, since that night.

I watched out my big bay window, as the sun went down.

I stared at the horizon. Watched the sun sink below the trees and houses of my little piece of suburbia.

Watched the shadows lengthen from the cars and trees and bushes along my block. Watched the dark begin to rise.

Because while morning might break, and light might fall, darkness rose.

Darkness, it lived beneath us. Always beneath us. Banished by our love of light.

It waited. Waited for us to let our guard down. Waited for the sun to sink.

Then, and only then, would the darkness rise. Fill all the spaces we told ourselves were blank. We told ourselves were empty.

I watched the darkness spread. Even as four teenagers down the block stumbled out a house in their rush to get wherever they were going on a Saturday evening. Laughing at each other. Laughing at themselves.

Or maybe just laughing.

They fell into their car. An old 90s station weapon. Peeled out like they were driving a Mustang.

All the time, unaware of the dark rising around them. Concealing dangers they couldn't guess at.

I found myself uttering a quick prayer that they would return home safely.

And I watched the dark rise until it settled. Held back as it was by the orange sodium street lights. The winking stars, and half-hiding moon.

They held a weak line though. Plenty of room for the darkness to spread.

Behind and under cars. Behind bushes. Trees. Even telephone poles.

Hidden places, where the darkness reigned.

I watched. Standing at my bay window. Empty glass gripped tight by white knuckles. Sweat on my brow. The sound of my own blood rushing past my ears.

Night time.

The time of the dark.

And yet, all over the world, people like those teenagers were laughing. Joking. Leaving their homes to go to movies. Concerts. Restaurants. Each other's houses.

Parks, even.

Treating the darkness not as a foe to respect and fear, but merely as a place waiting for more light. Waiting for *them* to bring more light.

Well, maybe it was time I ventured out. Joined the masses.

Maybe it was time I took back the night.

I had to get and down another glass of water first. Didn't taste it. Just needed it to get saliva flowing in my dry mouth again.

My skin was clammy, but I knew the night air would be warm.

Of course, I also knew my house was warm. But I told myself the night air would be good for me.

I would just walk down to the elementary school and back. Not even three blocks round-trip. Wouldn't take me fifteen minutes.

I put on socks and running shoes. Just in case.

I grabbed up my keys. Shoved them in the pocket of my cargo shorts. Did the same with my phone.

Wondered if I needed to grab anything else.

Caught myself starting back into the bedroom, to look for anything else I might "need."

Caught myself delaying.

I stepped up to my front door. The same front door I'd come back in through, not seven hours ago.

I clasped the cool doorknob. My grip tightened.

All I had to do was turn the knob. That was it. Just turn the knob. Open the door. Put one foot in front of the other.

Maybe I needed to change my shirt first. This Giants tee shirt was soaked now. All that cold sweat. Maybe I needed to comb my hair too.

That got me to laugh, still standing there, the doorknob tight in my grip.

My hair hadn't been long enough to comb since early high school.

I had everything I needed. Right there. Right now.

All I had to do was turn the knob.

Turn. The. Knob.

Turn.

The.

Knob...

I finally had to let go of the knob and fall back against the white wall, panting for breath. Sweat stinging my eyes. Heart pounding like I'd been trying to compete in an iron man without enough training.

I stared at the doorknob.

Damn it. No. I would do this. I could do this. I had to do this.

It was just the darkness. There was nothing out there in the darkness...

Or was there?

This was what it came down to.

This one thing was what it all came down to.

Five years of therapy. Three years of hiding.

And it all came down to this.

If I believed what the doctors all told me. If I believed that I'd had nothing more than a delusion. If I truly believed that, then I should be able to open that door and walk confidently out into the night.

No poachers or exotic animals in my neighborhood. Barely anything that could be called crime.

No. If I believed, then opening the door and stepping out into the evening air should have been the simplest act in the world.

So that was all I had to do, right?

I stepped up and grabbed the knob again. Tightened my grip. Squeezed like it was trying to wriggle away, and I needed to open the door while I could.

My hand began shaking.

Turn.

Turn the knob.

Turn the knob and admit that Page, Tangi and Todd died mundane deaths. The kind people died every day.

Turn the knob and admit it was all just bad luck. Being in the wrong place at the wrong time.

Turn the knob and admit that Mr. Xerxes was just a con man.

Turn the knob and admit, once and for all, that there was no vampire.

Turn the knob, damn it.

Find a life again.

Turn. That. Knob.

But I couldn't do it.

I got drunk that night.

Didn't take much, to be honest. I hadn't had a drop since the last time I'd gone drinking with Tangi.

But I had a twenty-one-year-old bottle of Glenmorton, that I'd been saving for the right occasion.

And this was definitely the right occasion.

I took my four tumblers over to the kitchen table. Poured a jigger of scotch into each glass. Added a touch of water to one, because that was what Todd would have wanted.

I raised my glass and said, "To the *Seekers*. We found the proof you'd always said we'd find. And it got you killed."

I drank then. And I kept drinking. And I kept toasting, too.

Each toast was a tribute. And an apology. And a confession.

I had eight years of denials to go through. So I was well and truly drunk by the time I'd gotten everything said.

Hell, I'm not even sure how intelligible those last toasts were.

I do know I got drunk though. More drunk than maybe I'd ever been before. Because I would have sworn — before I passed out, that is — that I actually saw the ghosts of my three friends in the kitchen with me.

They raised ghostly glasses, to toast the fact that I'd finally admitted the truth that the world had tried to make me deny.

I tried to drink that toast with them, but I passed out.

For the first time in years, I woke up well after the dawn.

In fact, it must have been close to noon. The hot sun was shining down through my kitchen window onto my face.

No hangover. I never got hangovers. Tangi used to hate that about me. Said I'd never had a proper drunk, if I'd never had a proper hangover.

So I may have woken up with a major case of cottonmouth, and I may have smelled like a whisky distillery, but my head wasn't pounding the way Tangi always said it should have been after a good night of drinking.

I did wake up on the linoleum of my kitchen floor though. Tangi would have been proud of that much.

I took a little time to clean up and change before making breakfast.

More cargo shorts — I had like six pairs of them — but the shirt, that was different.

I put on a *Seekers* tee shirt. Royal blue, with the show's logo done in white, and the text, "We will find the truth" on the back.

First time I'd worn one since, well, since I'd been part of the show.

I downed toast and orange juice, before I even went to wash my glasses from the night before.

I was embarrassed to realize I still had at least a half a bottle of Glenmorton left.

Man, I was a cheap drunk nowadays. All three of them would have laughed at me about that one.

I did pause for a moment when I saw that all four glasses were empty. Not just mine. I shook it off, at first, assuming that of course I'd just drunk their shares too, rather than waste good whisky.

None of them would have wanted me to waste good whisky.

But I stopped myself.

Made myself look at all four empty glasses.

If I ... if I was willing to admit to myself that my friends had been killed by a vampire — and clearly I was willing to admit that now — then why not believe that the ghosts of my friends had visited me last night?

All three of them sure as hell would have tried to contact me from beyond the grave. Todd and Page, for science. To prove it could be done. Tangi, he'd do it just for the chance to say goodbye.

I picked up all three glasses that had been "theirs." I tried to smell them, but I only smelled whisky residue.

"Bye, guys," I whispered. "Wish me luck. Because as soon as I eat breakfast, I'm going to try to finish what we started."

6

MR. XERXES PICKED UP ON THE FIRST RING. OF COURSE.

"Mr. Robertson?" he said, as though he'd been expecting my call. "Shall I presume you are calling because you are ready to talk?"

"No," I said. "I'm calling because I'm ready to do something about that fucking vampire."

"I'll just come over then, shall I?"

Didn't take him twenty minutes. He couldn't have been far away.

What surprised me, though, was that he didn't come alone.

Mr. Xerxes pulled up out front in an old Rolls Royce Phantom. Silver. In such good condition that it gleamed. Which made me wonder just how much his little "extranormal skills" put in his bank account on an annual basis.

But right behind him pulled up a motorcycle. Big, black beast. Maybe a thousand ccs, with low, simple handlebars, and a brown leather seat. Might have been an old Indian — before the name got purchased by another company — but I couldn't see any brand on the side.

The guy who got off the bike looked like he was the original owner.

His hair was gray as steel wool. Long, tied behind him in three places down his back. Skin tanned brown, but not many wrinkles. Scruffy. Not like he had a beard. More like he hadn't gotten around to shaving for several days.

He wore riding leathers that looked as old as his bike, but much, much more worn. They fit him like a second skin, and I had to admit, the old guy was in pretty darned good shape.

Bit of a belly, but at his age, he'd more than earned it. And he still had plenty of muscle.

He wore a plain gray tee shirt, under a leather vest that matched the pants.

Fingerless leather gloves on his hands competed the look.

He turned around to do something with the bike's seat, and I saw lettering on the back of his vest.

"Transmaniacon Motor Club." Underneath the words, which were done in gunmetal, was an upper torso and head look at the grim reaper, complete with hood and scythe.

My stomach fell. This guy was some kind of Hell's Angel?

What the hell was Mr. Xerxes doing bringing a Hell's Angel to my house?

I met them on my little red brick front porch.

"Um, hi?" I said as they came up the walkway together.

I had to admit, they looked comfortable with each other. Like they'd known one another for years. That might have relaxed me a bit, if I knew anything more about Mr. Xerxes than how he'd presented himself.

Mr. Xerxes didn't look like a biker. He wore a pale gray suit today, with pinstripes. And a matching bowler hat. He even walked with a diamond handled cane that I knew he didn't strictly need.

Then again, in my experience, anyone who chose a diamond handled cane, didn't *need* a cane.

"Excellent," Mr. Xerxes said, with what sounded to me like real happiness in his voice. "Eager to get started. Mr. Robertson, this is—"

"Des," the Hell's Angel said, holding out his hand. Veins of gold in his hazel eyes. "Call me Des."

"All right, Des," I said. "Then you'll have to call me Sel. You both should, really."

I shook hands with Des then, and dear God did this man have a grip. I would have sworn he wasn't even trying, but his hands could probably have crushed billiard balls.

I pulled back my aching hand just as Mr. Xerxes said, "A privilege, sir. And you must call me Edmund."

"Really ought to be Ed," Des said. He had a rough voice. Certainly rougher than his motorcycle's engine, which had been ghost-quiet as they'd approached.

Mr. Xerxes — Edmund — grimaced. "Please. Anything but that."

"Eddie?" Des said, with a broad grin. Good set of teeth too. Didn't know how old this guy was, but he sure looked healthy.

Edmund only cast a single raised eyebrow at his friend.

"Not Eddie then," Des said through a sigh. "Such a killjoy, Edmund."

"Shall we go inside?" Edmund asked me, pointedly ignoring his friend now.

"I don't ... really..." I sighed through my nose. "I don't think I have enough chairs."

"Then I'll sit on the floor," Des said with a shrug. "Wouldn't be a first. And it'll keep Eddie's — I mean *Edmund's* — suit clean."

"Fine," I said, chuckling now, as I stood aside and let them in.

"Dear dear," Edmund said, first through the door. "I can see we've only just arrived in the nick of time."

"You live like a beatnik," Des said, glancing around. "If beatniks watched television."

"Known many beatniks, have you?" I asked.

"Known a lot of everything, I'd say."

I didn't get to ask what he meant by that, because Edmund took charge.

"What I meant," he said in his normal, crisp tone, "was that you've already largely withdrawn from the world. Now, here, you're withdrawing from even yourself."

He turned and put a hand on my shoulder. Cool, despite the warm summer day.

"You cannot face the undead like this, Sel. Half a man cannot defeat the undead."

"Half a—"

"Means you're not whole," Des said. "He's not calling you a cripple. Physically anyway. But he does have a point." Des looked around. "Less of you in this room than there ought to be. Much time as you spend in here."

I felt the grimace. Felt the narrowing of my eyes. Felt the question burning at my lips. Instead, I asked the more basic, simple question.

"Des, if you don't mind my asking, just who the fuck are you?"

Edmund drew himself up, affronted.

But Des, he just laughed and slapped his knee.

"There! That's you. That question right there. More of you in that question than there is in this room, that's for sure."

"I assure you," Edmund said. "Des here is eminently qualified to—"

"I can speak for myself, Edmund. Hell, I've been doing it longer than you have."

Des looked me up and down, and that gaze had weight to it. I could feel it press against me.

Which made me think I was getting just a little too credulous. I'd have to watch that.

"Told you to call me Des," he said, "and that's more than enough name for now. As for who I am, who do you think I am?"

"I think you're a Hell's Angel. I think you're the muscle. Edmund here, he's brains in a way I'm not. Me, I think I'm probably brains in a way he's not. And I've got some muscle, but I'm not stupid enough to think I have enough muscle to go after a vampire alone."

I made a show of looking him up and down, though I knew my gaze didn't carry nearly as much weight.

"And you look like muscle to me."

"Not bad," Des said, raising one hand to still any comments from

Edmund. "Missed a little though. I'm not a Hell's Angel. Not the way you think of it. I do belong to a motor club. Obviously."

"Yeah," I said. "Just what the hell does 'transmaniacon' mean anyway?"

"As with understanding any word," Edmund said, "it's a simple matter of dissecting the parts. Trans-, a prefix meaning 'across or beyond.'"

"Beyond, in this case," Des said, "but keep going, Edmund."

"Mania, of course, is insanity."

"Madness," Des said. "Rings better. And -con?"

"Con, as a suffix, is, I believe, a reference to an older usage of the word. Knowledge. Thus, transmaniacon would be the knowledge beyond madness."

"See," Des said, giving me a big grin. "This is one of the reasons I keep Eddie around, no matter what he insists on being called. Damned good psychic, and a good, logical mind to boot. Don't see combinations like that much these days. Most psychics, whether they have anything on the ball or not, are those airy-fairy-farty types. Drive me nuts, with their new age yakking. Makes me want to—"

"We're not talking about Edmund right now," I said. "I've got a feel for who Edmund is. We're talking about who *you* are. And now I know what the name of your gang means, but I don't know anything else."

"Gang's a bit of a misnomer. The way you think of it, anyway. We're not criminals. We don't run drugs or guns or any of that. We're a motor club. We ride together as often as we can."

He sighed. "Unfortunately, I'm the only member around here right now. Because for a gig like this one, I definitely could use a few of the others along to help. Scott, Sean and especially Charles have all faced more vampires than I have."

"Fine," I said, exasperated at the double-talk. "Tell me this then. What is the knowledge you gained beyond madness?"

Des gave me another grin then, but this one looked ... old. Matched the look in his eyes in the moment. Older than anything else. Older maybe than this country. Centuries, in a single grin.

Just a flash, and then it was gone.

"That, my boy, you'd have to find out for yourself."

***

I FINALLY DRAGGED BOTH MY KITCHEN CHAIRS INTO THE LIVING ROOM. I got us each a glass of water, and set my little end table in the center, like a coffee table.

I did make apologies to Des for not having any beer. He volunteered to make a run, but Edmund wouldn't hear of it.

"We must have all of our faculties at our disposal, if we are to face the undead."

"Why do you keep calling it that?" I asked. "Why not just call it a vampire?"

"Does sound a bit pretentious. *Edmund.*"

"You must understand," Edmund said. "I prefer precision whenever possible. I believe it is true that what you faced — and what stalks you right now — is a vampire. That is consistent with both your experience and with what I have seen. But the problem with that word is that it brings with it a whole host of misunderstandings and assumptions."

"Does have a point," Des said, nodding. "Sel, when I say vampire, what do you think of?"

"Christopher Lee, in an evening suit and opera cape."

"Exactly so," Edmund said. "And so do very many others, across at least the United States, Canada, and Western Europe."

"More of 'em think of Brad Pitt these days," Des said. "Or James Marsters. Or maybe Robert Pattinson or—"

"Screen icons," Edmund said. "All of them."

"You specified Western Europe," I said. "Not Eastern Europe?"

"Most of the vampire legends that you've heard of come from Eastern Europe," Des said. "Say 'vampire' around there, and you have hundreds of years of folklore outweighing the influence of any one actor, or even any one author."

"What about Mexico?"

"It doesn't matter," Edmund said, giving both Des and me a look that I was pretty sure was meant to silence debate.

Des and I looked at one another. He nodded. I looked back at Edmund.

"My point is," Edmund said, "that the assumptions must be cleared, before we can bring real knowledge to the fore."

"Not strictly true," Des said, wiggling one hand back and forth. "My knowledge will be there one way or the other. Yours too, I expect. But—"

"If you'd both please," Edmund said, eyes closed in a long-suffering look. "We have only so many hours before sunset, and I would like to finish my point."

We both nodded at him.

"Misunderstandings and assumptions," Edmund said. "We *all* have them, and in the case of the undead, they can be perilous. Take, for example, the use of a wooden stake."

I started to mention that I knew a good lumberyard, but Edmund's raised eyebrow shut me up.

"For some vampires, any form of wood will suffice. For others, it is holly. Still others, oak. Or white hawthorn. Or black hawthorn. The possibilities, though not limitless, vary enough that attempting to wield a stake without the proper knowledge of the specific variety of undead you face will lead only to failure and your own death."

"How can the type of wood make that much difference?" I shook my head. "I'm sorry, Edmund, but it doesn't make sense. Wood pierces heart. Heart is destroyed. Even myths about creatures who hide their hearts in boxes and such, they all die if the heart is pierced. None of *them* care by what."

"And if we were facing Koschei the Deathless, then it would not matter what we used to pierce his heart."

"Whoa now," Des started, hands coming up. "If you find the heart of Koschei the Deathless—"

"Yes," Edmund said, raising the diamond handle of his cane. "I know. I would not be so foolish as to tempt fate by piercing the heart."

"Wait! Wait. Wait. Wait." I said, both my hands coming up too, but for entirely different reasons. "Who the hell is Kosh... Kasch..."

"Koschei the Deathless," Des said. "Russian Big Bad. Fought the Russian folk heroes. Even squared off with Baba Yaga from time to time."

"I'll thank you not to say *that* name in my presence," Edmund said.

"Why not?" I'm not sure who said that first. Me or Des. Or maybe we said it together.

"That is my business, and I do not choose to share it at this time."

"Wait," I said, trying again. "So you're telling me that these Russian folk monsters are all real and all out there?"

"I wouldn't use the word 'monsters' myself," Edmund said, "but yes."

"And that the *type* of wood matters?"

"If we attempt to use a stake, then of course the wood matters."

"How the fuck can it make a difference what type of wood we use? That's like saying that if you cut the head off wrong, it won't stay lopped off."

"And it might not," Edmund said, with more certainty in his voice than I thought that statement could merit. "Some such creatures would require a silvered blade for the decapitation to take. Others merely a blessed blade. Still others, a single blow."

"Or what?" I said. "The head grows back?"

"Reattaches," Des said, just as casually as though he'd been warning me about the scouting report on a team's running back. "Seen it happen."

"Bullshit." I shook my head. "How can that matter? You cut something off, it stays off."

Edmund sighed. Gave me an apologetic look.

"Forgive me, Sel, but you faced this creature before. Did you or did you not fire wooden bullets into it?"

"Well, yes, but—"

"And you hit the chest, did you not? At quite close range?"

"Well, *yes*, but—"

"And did any of these bullets slow it down?"

"Well, no, but—"

"I believe you also burned the creature with ultraviolet light. The same variety light used to simulate sunlight at tanning salons, and in sunlamps."

"We did, but—"

"And we know that also availed you not at all. So tell me this, Sel. Did the vampire cast a shadow?"

"There wasn't exactly a lot of light around there. It was just before dawn, and I was looking through my goggles."

"Not once the corpse of Todd Jeffries collided with you." Edmund's eyes seemed to bore through me. "As you lay on the ground, with the vampire standing over you, it stood between you and the moon. You should have been in shadow. Were you?"

"No," I said slowly. "I don't … think so. But I can't be sure."

"You can be sure of all of it," Des said. "The bullets. The light. The shadow. All of it."

"How do you know?"

"You asked about the knowledge that lies beyond madness." Des toasted me with his water glass. "I can hear truth. And what you said was true. Even if you aren't sure you believe it."

———

My living room was so still we might have been a photograph. The Hell's Angel, the man in the silk suit, and me, in a *Seekers* tee shirt and cargo shorts.

Even the breeze coming in through my kitchen windows seemed to be taking a break. But if it felt stifling just then, I couldn't have said.

Edmund sat motionless in my big recliner. Not looking at either of us, just then. His gray eyes stared at nothing.

Des stared at me, those veins of gold seeming to glow in his eyes. Anticipation in the air.

He was waiting for something. Another explosive swear word from me maybe. Cries of disbelief. Something.

All I gave him was a question.

"Just what the fuck does that mean? You can hear truth."

"Here it. Smell it. See it. Read it." Des shrugged. "Truth resonates. Falsehoods, they echo instead."

"What's the difference?"

"Qualitative. Hard to describe. It's like this. If you say something true, it has a depth, a weight to it. If you say something false, it lacks that weight. Try me. Say a few things."

"Fine," I said. "The first girl I slept with was Jenny Muldoon. Twelfth grade. She had the most amazing blond hair. All the way down to her waist."

I paused and looked at him.

He shrugged. "Waiting for something true."

I gritted my teeth. Jenny Muldoon was a brunette, all right, and her hair only fell down past her shoulders.

Wait.

"I did go with Jenny in the twelfth grade."

"Didn't sleep with her."

"She went down on me. That counts."

"This isn't the Congress, and you're not up for impeachment. She wasn't the first girl you slept with."

"If you're quite finished," Edmund said, sitting forward. "The time for parlor games has passed. Sel, you'll have to accept that what Des says he can do, he can do. What I say I can do, I can do. And we'll assume that what *you* say you can do, you also can do."

He looked from me to Des and back. "We must have faith in one another, to face the undead."

"All right then," I said. "You can remote view and use pendulums. And Des here is some kind of cosmic lie detector."

I couldn't help it. I turned to Des and said, without thinking, "The Giants will beat the Dodgers today. Truth or lie?"

Des grinned at me and shook his head, then downed the rest of his water.

"Doesn't work that way," he said. "There is no truth or falsehood there. Not yet."

"Please," Edmund said. "We must stay on topic."

I started to speak, but Edmund spoke louder. "I understand that this is difficult for you, Sel."

I frowned and sat back, trying to figure out how to say what I needed to say, but too many thoughts rushed through my head. They got jammed up on their way to my mouth.

Edmund organized his words before I could.

"I do understand," he said. "You are in the most difficult position of the three of us. I know it is not easy to see your understanding of the world stretch so far so fast. Not after years of seeking and not finding on your television show. Not after finding truth, only to have others demand that you deny this truth."

Edmund gestured at Des and himself with the diamond handle of his cane.

"And now here we come, forcing your eyes to widen until you see a world vaster than you would let yourself believe. Humor is a defense. Dismissive questions and the demands of your old world-view are a defense. Trying to cling to science on these subjects is a defense."

"Whoa," I said, forming a T with my hands. "Time out. Are you trying to say *science* doesn't apply here? *Science? Physics?*"

Edmund sighed. "Of course science applies. What you do not understand — and what most scientists deny when pressed by the larger world — is that science is limited."

"Come on," I said, and couldn't shake the feeling that my words *were* coming out as a defense mechanism. Which either went to show that he was getting into my head, or that maybe he had a point.

Either way, I pushed ahead. "Science either always works or it never works. It's not as though gravity's going to fail us at a critical moment, or like the speed of light is going to slow down when we're counting on it."

"I got this," Des said, raising one hand to Edmund. "Look. To continue with Eddie's larger-world analogy, look at it this way. Most people, they only look at what's right in front of them. They have peripheral vision that covers almost a hundred and eighty degrees but still, they only really watch maybe forty-five degrees. Ninety at the most. Are you with me so far?"

I nodded, eyes narrowed. I wasn't sure I liked where this was going.

"Right," he said with a nod. "Science does a badass job of shining a bright light into that forty-five degrees, dig? Lights it up like a mall on Black Friday. But their beam, it's pretty tight. The people who can see ninety degrees, they see more shadows than anything else. And they want to see clearly."

I stared making a move-this-along motion with my hand, but that just made Des chuckle.

"Now the people who see those shadows? Some of them are scientists, looking to widen the beam of light. Others are philosophers and magicians, finding their own way in the shadows."

Des raised one finger. "But there's still the matter of the rest of that one-eighty, still in darkness."

"Plus," I said, voice brimming with sarcasm, "God forbid someone turns around."

Des slapped his knee and laughed.

"You think you're joking, but you're not. See, I'm a guy who's spun in circles. That's what I'm talking about by transmaniacon. Edmund here, he's the sort who sees the whole one-eighty in front of him. And you, you my boy are just starting to see into the shadows."

I sighed and shook my head. "But that doesn't explain how science doesn't work in some places. Light is still light."

"Simple," Des said. "Science is the best way in the world to analyze something and figure it out. That's all it really is, you know. A set of rules to follow when studying something, that try to get the operator out of the way, so he doesn't muck up the findings with his expectations."

"Which limits it," Edmund said, "because it cannot predict responses from areas it has not studied. Not with any degree of accuracy."

"Plus," Des added, "once you get out into the shadows, let alone the darkness, you'll find more and more things that *must* be affected by the operator. It's both their nature, and the nature of the universe itself."

"If either of you tries to claim this is proof of quantum mechanics or something—"

"Stop," Edmund said with a sigh. "Try that route, and you miss the point. Quantum mechanics is an attempt to study the shadows while the beam of light begins to broaden. It has no way of predicting what will be found in the shadows, let alone the darkness."

I downed about half my water glass then. Mostly for a break. A chance to try to absorb what they were telling me. And Des and Edmund, they seemed to realize that. Because they waited for me to speak again.

The moment I saw that happening, I stretched out that time to think by taking our glasses — well, two of them, because Edmund had yet to touch his water — into the kitchen for refills.

I tried to organize my thoughts. What I knew. What I'd seen on *Seekers*, even apart from that one night. All the things Todd and Page used to say.

Tangi and me, we were techies, in the world of film and television. Him with his camera and me with my mics. Neither one of us went into the theory behind the equipment. At least, not more than we needed in order to understand how it worked, and how to jury-rig repairs in the field.

I might have come a little closer, learning enough about the physics of sound that I could build my own studio, complete with soundproofing.

But Todd and Page, *they* were the scientists. Parapsychologists. And they were sticklers for how they handled data. How they approached their studies. They used to say that parapsychology was so derided as a science that it got held to stricter standards than any other discipline. That they needed ten times as much proof, with ten times as many precautions, to get as much credit for their work as a physicist.

But Todd and Page were dead.

They were dead because all their science failed in the face of the undead. The vampire. Whatever the fuck that thing was.

It ... I hated to continue that analogy, but that vampire was a creature of the darkness. And Todd and Page had only gotten as far as into the shadows.

That was the truth...

Or was it?

It was one thing to believe in a vampire I'd actually fought. Saw it get shot without caring. Felt its strength when it threw Todd's body into me.

But what they were saying, it went way beyond the idea that there was one vampire out there...

I carried the two glasses of water back into the living room.

Handed Des his glass, and stood right in front of him. Stared hard into those eyes, with their golden veins standing out more right now than their hazel.

Des, he raised his steel wool eyebrows and looked back at me.

"I have one question for you. No. I have one thing I want to say. And I want you to tell me if it's true or false. If you can't, I'm done here. If I think you're lying or bluffing, I'm done here."

Edmund drew breath, but I forestalled him with a raised hand, without ever looking away from Des.

"Do you agree?" I asked him.

"Sure," he said with a nod. "I get the feeling you need to know."

"Todd and Page could see into the shadows. They died because they couldn't see far enough."

"Yep," he said, without a moment's hesitation. And in that moment, I saw age in his eyes again. Vast age. Centuries.

But he was still talking, soft and intent. "That's the truth, Sel. Your friends were whip-smart. Make no mistake. They were ready for anything they could have imagined. But what they found, that was outside their imaginations."

"But—"

"No," Edmund said. "He's right, Sel. They were limited by their thinking. And the undead told you as much."

That slammed a dozen things together in my head at the same time.

I fell backward. Stumbled across the oak end table. I would have hit the floor, but Des' strong hand darted out and caught me.

He stood, easily controlling my not insignificant weight with one hand, and eased me into my chair.

I just sat there blinking.

And Des and Edmund, they gave me that time.

In the distance, I heard too many ordinary things. Sounds of everyday life, filtering in through the kitchen windows, along with the gentle breeze.

A lawnmower, down the street. Cars passing. Kids yelling to each other. A plane flying past overhead. Lower than it should have been.

The heat of the day, a normal thing. Seasonal. No hotter than yesterday. Maybe not even as hot.

My stomach, it quivered, not quite ready to rumble, but letting me know that eating soon would be welcome.

So ordinary. So everyday. I had a glass of water in my hand. Sipped a little. Good tap water. Cool, but not cold, trickling into my mouth, then down my throat as I swallowed. I could feel it reaching my stomach.

Good things. Normal things. Everyday things.

But ... they weren't everything. That was a lie.

No. But they weren't the whole truth either.

No.

I...

I couldn't quite put it together. Frowned with my whole face. Searching for how to say what I was thinking. What I was feeling.

"Breathe," Des said.

I realized then he'd moved the end table. He was kneeling before me. Looking up at me. Hands raised, as though he thought I might fall off the chair and he might have to catch me.

"Slow and easy," he said, and he fell into a soothing cadence as he continued. "One breath, before you worry about the next. Just take that warm summer air in deep until it feels like it fills you down to your sandals. Then let it back out, just as slowly."

He gave me three breaths that way before he spoke again.

"You asked for truth," Des said. "But truth is a hard thing. Especially to a man in your position. You've lived in the center of the light. Your friends looked into the shadows, but you didn't look with them. Then the darkness leapt in front of you."

He eased his voice into a more normal cadence, and it seemed to start bringing me back to myself, as he continued.

"Then you were forced back into the light. Your life has been fragmented. That's why you've lived the way you have. And now, you're getting the missing puzzle pieces. Things are snapping into place for you. The next few days, few weeks, they'll be tough."

"Unfortunately," Edmund said, "we can't just give them to you." He sighed. "If we could, I would have Des and myself go away for two weeks or so. Return to you then, when your psyche has had time to properly adjust. But we don't have that time."

"He's right," Des said, standing now. "Given my druthers, I'd definitely let you work things out. Maybe meet me once a week or so to answer more questions for you. Let you adjust."

Des shook his head.

"Why is this so urgent now?" I asked, starting to feel more like myself again. Even though my stomach was churning. "What's changed?"

"Two weeks ago," Edmund said, "you did a job down in Half Moon Bay."

"Yeah," I said. "The tide pool thing. All shot by noon, and I was home in plenty of time. Why?"

"Much as we have allies, so does the undead. One of those allies spotted you." Edmund's head bobbed back and forth. "Or so I believe. I cannot be certain. I was viewing—"

"Be certain," Des said. "It's the truth."

Edmund frowned at Des. "Why didn't you tell me before?"

"Didn't matter," Des said with a shrug. He sat down again. "We were coming here to do what needed doing."

"Well," Edmund said, one eyebrow raised and still a bit of a grimace on his face, "the point is that the undead now knows where to find you."

"How?" I said. "I mean, how could this ally recognize me? Why would he or she or it or whatever, even be looking for me?"

"That is less certain," Edmund said, then raised an inquisitive eyebrow at Des.

"Sorry," Des said. "That's not a simple truth-falsehood situation. There are too many factors involved for me to taste it properly."

"Taste?" I said.

"Metaphor," Des said.

"In any event," Edmund said. "We must determine the nature of the undead, before we can go after it. And we must go after it soon, or we risk it choosing the time and place of the attack."

"So we need information," I said. "Information that you two can't get on your own."

"Essentially, yes," Edmund said. "And if we knew how and why you survived, that would be movement in the right direction."

"And you say the vampire — the *undead* — is close?"

"Very," Des said. "Pretty sure he's in town right now."

"It," Edmund insisted. "Do not humanize the creature."

"Then I know what we need to do."

Both of them looked so puzzled I couldn't help but laugh.

"We have to go back to Missouri. To that cemetery."

"Its home has moved since then," Edmund said.

"But the answers to how I survived have to be there."

Edmund looked at Des, who smiled.

"Boy's got a point. There's a reason you saw what you saw, and I think all roads are leading us to Springfield."

"Well, outside it, anyway."

"You can get us back there?"

"I'll have to."

"Then let us begin," Edmund said, standing.

Des joined him in almost the same instant.

I hesitated.

"It's all right," Des said softly. "You're going to have to go out at night to do this."

"Fuck that," I said. "Night is when this thing is at its most powerful."

"We don't know that for certain," Edmund said. "It may be just as powerful in the daytime, though more restricted in its movements."

"And that means, less powerful." I shook my head. "We're going to need to operate in the daytime until we're ready to fight this thing. You both need to realize that."

"I won't cower at night like a..." Des broke off and looked at me. "Sorry, but I don't have the reasons for it that you do. Maybe you need to stay inside at night, but I don't. And I won't."

"We need to travel," Edmund said. "If we leave now and catch a flight soon, we should be in Missouri by tonight."

"Which means, outside after dark." I shook my head. "Nope. We won't be able to chase things down at night anyway. Not without risking..."

I shook my head again. "Look. You guys just admitted that all the bad things that go bump in the night, they're all real. Let's respect that. We'll buy our tickets for an early flight tomorrow, and be in Springfield well before nightfall tomorrow."

Edmund drew breath with objection in his eyes, but Des stopped him with a hand on the shoulder.

"He needs time, Edmund. This is a lot. Give him tonight."

Des then turned to me and said, "You'll need to go out at night again. I'm hoping we can handle things in the daylight, but you can't be useless at night, or this could all blow up in our faces."

Des didn't wait for me to have a rejoinder then. He turned and started prompting Edmund to precede him out the door.

"What about the tickets?" I said.

"I'll handle everything," Edmund said. "Be ready for a cab to pick you up at daybreak tomorrow."

"All right. See you then."

They said their goodbyes, and I closed the door after them.

I leaned against the door. Realized I was holding a breath and let it out.

Vampires were real. And not just vampires.

"Todd, Page," I said, eyes heavenward. "Wherever you guys are now, I owe you a big apology."

PREPPING FOR THIS TRIP TOOK LESS TIME THAN I THOUGHT. IT WAS summertime, so my cargo shorts and tee shirts would be more than enough. I could just stuff them, along with underwear and socks, into a duffle bag and still have plenty of room for the basic necessities of life.

Meant I had a mostly empty backpack. I almost figured I wouldn't need it, but I'd have to carry weapons somehow. And I had the feeling Des and Edmund would be able to come up with weapons more useful in this case than anything Page every dreamed up.

And I suspected I'd do a lot of the hefting.

Once that was done, it was just a matter of calling work for the time off. And given that I'd taken exactly zero time off in my three years of working there, my boss was thrilled to give me two weeks to do whatever I wanted with. More if I needed it.

Apparently HR had been riding him about my lack of time off. I apologized for that, because, well, it felt right.

Plus, I'd been apologizing a lot that day.

I went for another run in the afternoon sun, just to get some good endorphins flowing through my system. Not to mention I expected I'd need to run before all this was over, and training was never a bad idea.

Besides, it was what I did whenever I felt off-kilter in life. Just one of the reasons I'd gotten so good at it.

So, after maybe a dozen miles of suburbia I got back, showered, ate a light dinner, and got ready to watch the night rise.

I didn't do it every night, but that night, I needed to do it again.

Especially now that I knew what I knew about shadows and darkness. Made the rise of night seem even more sinister.

I stopped that flow of thoughts as the Sunday evening darkness spread along my street. As the kids of the neighborhood all reached their homes via bikes or cars. Slammed doors on their way in for Sunday dinner.

And not just the kids. Visitors arrived to some of the houses, while at others, the denizens went out. Visiting or something else.

I stopped the flow of worry about shadows and darkness, though, because of one thing Edmund and Des hadn't mentioned.

Maybe everywhere outside the light was darkness, but that didn't mean it was all evil.

Sure, vampires were evil. And a whole host of other things were too.

But angels, didn't they have to be real too?

And what did that say about God?

I hadn't been to church in a number of years, but as the darkness rose, I found myself kneeling in prayer at my big bay window that night.

"God," I said, "if You're listening, thank You for saving me from the vampire all those years ago. I wish You'd saved my friends too, but I've heard about Your mysterious ways, and I'm trying not to take it personally."

I grimaced at that. I was pretty far out of practice at prayer. I tried to think of what to say as I knelt there, hands folded in front of me and eyes closed.

Finally, I just let the words come out.

"I'm angry at You for that, God. I'm angry that You let this vampire exist. I'm angry that You let it kill my friends."

I drew a few breaths and counted to ten then. No point in just railing at the Almighty.

"But, God, I'm going to try to kill that thing. And I'm probably going to need Your help to do it. Yeah, I know. God helps those who help themselves. But I'm doing this. Me, and Des, and Edmund. And this vampire, it's an abomination. It needs to be ended. Even if it decided tonight to go away and leave me alone, I'd still need to kill it.

"But, God, we both know it won't do that. For some reason, it wants to finish me off. So I *need* to kill it before it kills me."

I was running out of steam awfully fast here, so I drew one more deep breath and tried again.

"So, God, if You're listening. Please bless Edmund, Des and me as we try to kill an abomination that You allow to exist. Please keep us safe, and let us slay the thing that is out there right now, killing Your children.

"If the human race means a damn to You and Your infinite wisdom, then bless us and keep us safe as we try to destroy what You should never have allowed to exist in the first place. Amen."

I started to rise up, but then had another thought.

"And, God, if You have any advice for this poor sinner about how to kill this vampire and survive doing it, I'd love to hear it."

I stayed there kneeling for a while. Listening.

I could hear the evening breeze in the trees outside. I could hear the television across the street. Not clearly, just the sound of whatever sporting event they were watching. The Giants-Dodgers game, maybe.

I could hear cars in the distance. The horn of a train.

But if God had anything to say to me, I couldn't hear Him.

Still, praying may have done me *some* good. The vampire didn't come for me that night.

7

Up before dawn, even earlier than usual that next morning. Showered, shaved, and dressed in dark gray cargo shorts and another *Seekers* shirt. This one white with a royal blue logo.

I ate a good breakfast of fried eggs and toast, with lots of bacon and orange juice.

All right, I was half clearing out my pantry before leaving, since I might never return.

I tried not to think about it that way, even if the idea was lurking in the back of my mind.

I tried to tell myself I was just fortifying for a long day of travel.

By the time the cabbie honked for me, just as the first rays of dawn filtered into my kitchen, I almost believed it.

And the day of travel turned out not to be as long as I expected, to be honest.

The cabbie brought me not to the main Sacramento airport, but a smaller, satellite airport. Which had me worried at first. The last thing I wanted to do was ride a puddle-jumper for six hours.

But no, the cab drove straight out onto the tarmac, and stopped beside a private jet.

Oh, it wasn't a 747 or anything. It wasn't just a little Honda personal plane, either. It was somewhere between the two. And from the loud whine of its engines, it was gassed up and ready to go.

The cabbie refused my offer of a tip, which had never happened to me before. Especially not from a guy like this one. This cabbie looked grizzled and old. Had a voice that spoke of forty years of smoking, and a face so lined it was hard to believe his short curls were still more black than gray.

Nevertheless, he held up a hand to stop me and said, "Believe me, I've already gotten my tip on this fare."

I almost asked what he meant, but given that Edmund arranged it, either it was a lot of cash, or remote viewing. Either way, I probably didn't want to know. I just grabbed my bags and got out.

There were portable stairs — the kind on wheels — positioned to lead up into the private jet. Still, I wasn't sure I was in the right place.

"Hello?" I called up.

Edmund came to the door and smiled down at me. He was wearing gray pinstripes today, with a jaunty white cravat. He was also smiling wider than I'd seen him do yet.

"Good morning, Sel," he said and waved. "Come aboard. We're ready to go, and we have clearance."

I hustled up the stairs, flashing on a memory of being in high school and having to run up and down the bleachers as part of my training. Hadn't done it since high school, but it was a good workout.

If I survived this mess, I might work it back into my schedule.

Edmund met me with a handshake, then stepped back and gestured me inside.

Eight total seats, and they looked like they rotated. And room for many, many more. These weren't regular, confining airline seats either. These were practically as big as my recliner at home, and they looked as though they might tilt backward even farther.

Thin brown carpeting. White walls. The rest of it looked more like a normal airplane cabin. Except that there were ... footlockers? I wasn't sure what else to call them. There were about eight of them all together, four down along the — hull? What does one call the walls of plane? — on each side.

"Just what kind of plane is this, anyway?"

"Cessna Citation Hemisphere," Edmund said, pride in his voice. "My biggest indulgence. But at my age, the less time I waste in airports, or packed in tightly amid the masses of humanity, the better I feel."

"Just how much money do you make?"

"A gauche question, Sel," Edmund chided me. "I'd expect you to know better. Suffice to say that I am willing to bring all of my weapons to bear on this task. There's no point in wealth, if I die trying to scrimp."

Des came out of the back of the plane, dusting his hands. Or maybe getting water off of them, if he'd been in the bathroom.

He was dressed pretty much the way I'd seen him yesterday, down to the gray tee shirt.

"Good," Des said. "Prompt. Figured you would be."

"I'll tell the captain," Edmund said, and stepped to the front of the plane as I moved in to wince as I shook Des' hand.

"A private jet?" I whispered.

"What?" Des said with a smile. "You don't have one?"

"And I suppose you do?"

"That would be telling."

Des took my bags and stowed them in one of the compartments I thought of as a footlocker.

Edmund came back and joined us, then the three of us were strapped in and the jet took off.

Smooth flight. There was even a stewardess, to bring us drinks and snacks and lunch.

And then we were on the tarmac in Springfield, almost before I knew it.

Might have helped that we discussed our plans along the way. Gave me something to focus on.

Apart from the plans, I even had time for one question. One that had been nagging at me since before I prayed last night.

"If there's supernatural evil in the world," I started.

Edmund finished. "Is there good?"

"Sort of," Des said. "The thing about good, is it tends to be focused on individual choices and free will. So, good isn't likely to jump in and save your bacon at the eleventh hour."

"It *can* happen," Edmund said.

"It's not likely though."

Edmund cleared his throat gently. Nodded to me.

"You think *I'm* supernatural good?" I said with a laugh.

"No," Des said, grinning at me, "he's pointing out that someone or something saved *your* bacon at the eleventh hour on that big night eight years ago. We don't know what or who, but dollars to donuts it was supernatural aid."

"And what it was is something we must discover," Edmund said, bringing us back into our planning session.

We landed right on schedule, apparently. Didn't even need to circle a few times before landing.

Then we taxied to a stop, and our stewardess opened the door.

A blast of familiar hot air.

I was back in Missouri in the summertime, and I remembered why I hated it the moment that door was open.

Wasn't any hotter there than it was back in Rancho Verde. But the humidity made it much, much worse.

How Edmund could stand it in those silk suits, I'd never understand.

Anyway, at the bottom of the roller stairs, a private car was waiting to bring two of us to the hotel Edmund had arranged. The Usher, over in east Springfield. A swankier hotel than I ever got to stay in before.

Oh, and I should say a car was waiting to bring *two* of us to the hotel, because one of us wasn't taking the car.

No. One of us had a bike waiting for him.

His bike.

I stared slack-jawed at it. "How?"

Des grinned at me. "Knowledge beyond madness. Comes in handy."

SPRINGFIELD DIDN'T FEEL LIKE A CITY TO ME. I MEAN, IT HAD BUILDINGS, and homes, and was spread out over a decent-sized piece of land, it's just...

I was a California boy. Springfield felt like a suburb, without a bigger city attached. That was the only way I could really put it.

Certainly, it didn't seem to be a big enough city to rate a hotel like the Usher.

The Usher wasn't a chain though. There had to be some kind of local concern that brought people in. Branson maybe. Tangi would have known. I felt a wistful wish that I could have asked him, as we cruised through the streets to our hotel.

Twenty stories, and with nothing else so tall around it, the hotel looked enormous. Glass and steel construction, but it wasn't a rectangle. It looked more like a rectangle that had started to slide from the top, so the rest of the building just kind of went with it.

Looked unstable. Probably never would have been allowed in earthquake country. But we weren't in earthquake country now. I wondered how it would handle a tornado.

Above the fifteenth floor, even from the car I could see broad balconies of concrete, painted to blend in with the skyline.

Even the hotel lobby of the Usher was fancier than anything I'd ever seen. I immediately felt underdressed. Classical music played softly in the background — and not piped in. An actual quartet of musicians with stringed instruments provided the soundtrack.

Both temperature and humidity were regulated the moment the doorman closed the glass lobby doors behind us, and the bellhop was already bringing our bags to our room before we'd even checked in.

And to check in, we didn't go to a front desk. Oh, no. A beautiful young woman with auburn curls met us along an actual stretch of red carpet, and checked out reservation on her tablet. Took her all of five seconds to verify us, get us our keys, wish us a happy stay and get out of our way.

Scary efficient. Was this was real money was like?

The elevator was perfumed with a hint of sage. Either that, or the previous occupants had been. The elevator was mirrored, but the gentle lighting somehow made even my reflection flattering.

And honestly, I hadn't smiled at my reflection in years.

Not that I did it in the elevator. But standing there, looking at the reflections of the three of us, I could have smiled.

We didn't have a room at the Usher. We had a suite. With four bedrooms, even though we only needed three. There was a large living area, with a bigger flatscreen television on the wall than I had at home, and enough seating for a decent super bowl party.

My bags were waiting in my room. How the bellhop decided which room was mine, I didn't want to know. Mine had an eastern view though. And before I even checked out the California king bed or the other amenities, I had to stop and stare out the window.

I tried to find an angle that would see the old road we'd driven that night. See if I could find clues that would help me figure out where we were headed. How to find that cemetery again.

I suddenly realized I hadn't taken a breath in over two minutes. I'd been standing there as though expecting something to erupt out at me. Even though it was safe to say I was someplace that ought, at least, to be vampire-proof. If anyplace was.

I gave the rest of my room a quick check. Huge bathroom with misting, multi-nozzle shower. More couches. Another big television. A huge desk, if I wanted to check anything on my laptop.

A half-sized refrigerator, complete with bottles of water and soda labelled *compliments of the Usher*.

I just had time to grab a bottle of water before Edmund called us all back into the main room.

From there, we three split up to begin our local research.

We checked out a few things around Springfield while the sun was still in the sky. Des got us police reports. I got my own records from the hospital. Edmund made contact with a few people he knew locally, thanks to what little presence he did maintain online.

None of the people Edmund knew were willing to step up and help. That seemed to irritate him, but it didn't surprise me.

"They're just happy the vampire's out of their state," I said. "They don't want me back here if it'll bring it back, and they don't want its attention."

"Nevertheless," Edmund said. "I will remember those who chose not to help, when their help was needed."

We were discussing this at a light dinner in the hotel restaurant.

The hotel restaurant was open and airy, with plenty of those plants that don't need dirt to grow. They were in dirtless glass bubbles held on nearly invisible wire, at different heights, under the high glass ceiling.

The tables were intimate, even four-tops like ours, and spaced enough for at least the illusion of privacy.

We weren't the only diners, either. And I was the worst-dressed person here.

Well, me or Des, at least. We were the only men not in suits. And the women were all in dresses that looked like they cost more than my car.

Broader range of ages than I expected, too. I figured a place with swank would appeal to the, well, Edmunds of the world. But there were plenty of other diners in their thirties and below.

And not all of them were staying here. I could tell by the fact that they stared around in even more slack-jawed awe than I did. They looked almost as though they wanted to apologize for being here.

At least, until they got a look at me. Then their expressions soured like there wasn't enough cream in their coffee.

I threw them smiles whenever I caught their glares. I used to get the same kind of reaction at my parents' country club, when I was a kid. I didn't take shit from those people then, and I wasn't about to start now.

"Ignore them," Des said. "This is all they have. You have a lot more."

I didn't know what to say to that. But Edmund saved me from replying by saying, "I trust the two of you did better than I?"

"Well," I said with a sigh. "It's nothing I haven't read before." I put my file on the table. "Maybe you two can see something in it that I can't. My throat was torn open. I'd suffered a serious blow to the head. I'd lost a lot of blood. Yadda yadda yadda."

"May I see it?" Edmund asked. He was dining on filet of salmon with risotto, but he wanted to look at a medical file.

I shrugged and handed it to him. I supposed I didn't have any room to complain. I was eating a rib eye, very rare, with garlic smashed potatoes and asparagus shoots. Then again, it was *my* file.

Des was eating a burger and fries. That the waiter hadn't *actually* scowled, in my opinion, meant he deserved an even better tip than he was going to get anyway.

"I had better luck," Des said. "There was an anonymous call to 911. That was how they happened to find you in the first place. Can't be sure who placed it, but it was an old woman's voice. Should help us narrow the options a bit."

"And just how, exactly, did you find this out?"

"My connections are reliable," Des said, and took a huge bite out of his burger.

"Here's something interesting," Edmund said, after finishing a bite of salmon. "It says you had dirt on your face."

"Well," I said, "I *did* fall in a cemetery."

"True," he said, nodding, "but the dirt was only on your forehead. Just above the nose. It also says here that you had three black feathers in your pocket."

"Yeah, that's got to be wrong. I don't go around picking up feathers."

"Wha' ki' o' fea-ers?" Des asked, barely comprehensible around his bite of burger.

"Chicken. Black chicken feathers."

"Yeah, I don't know..." I realized that Des and Edmund were giving each other a significant look.

"Three black chicken feathers," Des said, after swallowing. "And graveyard dirt on his forehead."

"Well, cemetery," I said, but they weren't listening to me.

"Hoodoo, you think?" Edmund asked.

"Voodoo?" I said, trying to catch up.

"Not Vodou," Des said. "Hoodoo. Folk magic."

"Wait," I said, thinking hard now. Those broken mason jars. "Page said something about Ozark folk magic. Some broken—"

"Mason jars?" Des said, then when I nodded he broke into a grin.

"Okay," he said. "An old woman called 911. And someone used a kind of folk magic — possibly Hoodoo, but we don't know for sure yet — to either protect you or keep you alive."

"Or both," Edmund said. "No reason it had to be just one."

"So," I said, "does that give you guys a better idea of who we're looking for?"

Des and Edmund both smiled. And Des' smile looked almost feral.

"We're not going now," I said.

"But—" Edmund started, but Des raised a hand to stop him.

Des looked at me. "Too close to dusk?"

"Gonna take us three hours to get out there," I said. "In all likelihood." I shook my head. "Not tonight."

Edmund let out an impatient breath. "You realize, the creature will feed tonight. Wherever it is currently, it will feed."

"What do you mean, wherever it is?" I said. "I thought you said it was in Rancho Verde."

"And if we knew what manner of undead it was," Edmund said patiently, "then I could tell you that with certainty. All I know at the moment is that it *was* in Rancho Verde, California, yesterday."

"What difference—"

"There are some," Des interrupted me, "that can track a chosen target, once they get a … feel for it. If it's that kind, then it may already be following you."

"But we left in daylight."

"And if it needs only shelter from the sun," Edmund said, "and not to lie in torpor awaiting nightfall, then it might be here in Spring-field by now."

"But—"

"Can't assume it doesn't have slaves," Des said.

"Slaves?" I said.

"Yes," Edmund said. "Some varieties don't merely dine on their prey. They subvert the will of some chosen individuals, and force them to serve their undead master as its daytime guardians. Perhaps even as its literal eyes and ears at times."

I dropped my silverware. My stomach puckered. I began to taste bile. Had to swallow it down. Chugged some water to help.

Edmund's eyes widened. "Oh dear."

"You think..." Des let his words trail off.

I needed to say those words though. I couldn't leave them unspoken.

"That might be what happened to Page. Or Tangi." I swallowed again. "Or both."

I didn't go out that night. Obviously.

Edmund and Des chased down a few more contacts. Did a little more research. But I just stayed up there in my room once the sun was below the horizon.

I wasn't a hundred percent certain that a hotel room could keep me safe from a vampire. Both Des and Edmund agreed that it might, depending on the type.

But everything depended on the type.

I had to trust that it would. Or that the vampire wouldn't be here. Not yet.

I didn't get much accomplished with our research though.

I was too busy getting lost in thought.

More than eight years now since that night.

More than eight years that Page and Tangi might have been slaves of the thing that definitely killed Todd.

I wasn't sure which was worse. Being food for that thing, or its…

No. I knew which was worse.

I prayed again that night. I prayed that Page and Tangi were dead, and not the bound slaves of that unholy monster. I prayed that their ghosts really had visited me, and that it meant that their bodies were dead and their souls were free.

Once again, though, if God heard me, he gave no sign.

8

I HAD A ROUGH NIGHT. DIDN'T GET A WHOLE LOT OF SLEEP, AND WHAT sleep I got was plagued with the worst kind of dreams.

I couldn't call them nightmares. Not really. I was used to thinking of nightmares as being ways my mind dealt with stress. Coming to work naked, showing up late and unprepared for a test, nuclear war interrupting a date, zombies hitting the family reunion.

Yeah, I'd had all those.

My dreams that night though, they were worse. I kept hearing Page's scream. That last sound that I ever heard from her. But in the dream, I heard Tangi screaming too. And Todd's severed head kept blaming me. Said I was too slow on the draw. That if I'd shot straight, he'd've lived.

All of them saying that if I'd only believed, we would have all lived through that night.

And just before the six times I jolted awake in a cold sweat?

That vampire's laugh.

Should have been a low, menacing laugh. Something James Earl Jones would portray.

Should have been, but not. The sound was ... kind of a hillbilly laugh. A gut-splitter, with odd octave leaps in the center of it. And a rough quality. Like it was rusty. Like it was a sound that the vampire hadn't made in many, many years. And it almost didn't remember how.

That, that was the sound that kept waking me up.

It chilled me to the bone, every time.

I kept turning the heat in my bedroom up — each room of the suite had its own temperature control, including the bathrooms — but it never seemed to help.

Finally, I gave up, showered and got dressed about an hour before dawn. Khaki cargo shorts, running shoes, and a blue *Seekers* shirt with the white logo.

I wandered into the main room of the suite, to see that Edmund was already awake and fully dressed. Well, his jacket was hanging in the corner, but otherwise he was already wearing a navy blue silk suit, with a crisp white shirt, gold cuff links, and a lavender tie.

He was even wearing perfectly shined shoes.

At about five in the morning.

He sat at the big table in the main room, near the wet bar. The table was a rectangular beast that must have weighed four hundred pounds and could have sat eight. It had a dark wood frame, and two heavy panels of glass forming most of the top.

Edmund's hands were neatly folded on the edge of the table. His eyes were closed. His breathing, slow and deep. I might have thought he was asleep, but he didn't seem the type to sleep in a common area.

Had to be meditating. Or remote viewing, I supposed.

I went over to the phone on the spare desk, near the three huge, windows, and the glass door that led out onto the suite's patio. I picked up the handle to dial the operator and ask what time the restaurant opened.

I never got as far as pushing a button.

Just before the handset reached my ear, Edmund said, "The restaurant does not open for two hours. I have already ordered us room service. I trust you wish something along the lines of standard American breakfast fare?"

"Does it come with lots of bacon, orange juice and coffee?"

"Of course."

"Good enough for me," I said, and joined him at the table. "Did you sleep like that?"

"No," he said, finally opening his eyes. "I've been trying for the past hour to remote view the undead. Something must be blocking me."

"What could do that?"

"Difficult to say with certainty," he said, then shook his head. A small, economical gesture. "The option I like least is that the creature is sensitive enough to detect my efforts, and clever enough to foil them."

"Clever enough?"

"Make no mistake," Des said through a yawn as he entered from his own room. His steel wool hair was a mess, and he was dressed only in a fluffy white robe with the name of the hotel monogrammed above his heart. He stretched, then finished his thought as he ambled over to join us. "The beast will be cunning. Intelligent may not be the right word, but cunning definitely is."

"What's the difference?" I asked.

Edmund spoke, as Des turned a chair around and plopped onto it.

"Intelligence is what humans possess, as well as certain of the higher orders of spirits. It can be directed toward all manner of problems, both real and imagined. It is capable of beauty as well as ugliness, and wonder as well as horror."

Edmund drew a sharp breath through his nose.

"Cunning, as applied to the undead and the lower orders of spirits, means an effective intelligence, oriented entirely around its purpose. In the case of the undead, that purpose is survival and hunting. Preying on humans."

"What, functionally, is the difference to us?" I asked.

"Simple," Des said. "If it's intelligent, we can reason with it. Get it to understand other perspectives. Learn to approach its problems from directions that go beyond simple survival. Might even adopt a live-and-let-live policy."

"Like, say, learning to raid blood banks instead of dining on living people?"

"I would have said working with willing donors in small doses," Edmund said. "For there have always been those drawn to the undead, who would spill blood for them."

"Point's the same," Des said, yawning again, which brought a yawn out of me as he continued. "If it were intelligent, we might not have to kill it."

"Yes, we would," I said. "It killed Todd, and likely killed Page and Tangi, if it didn't do worse to them. It dies."

"Careful there," Edmund said sharply. "You must learn to temper your emotions."

"Bullshit," I said. "I'm running on anger and revenge right now, because I'm sure as hell not running on sleep."

And it was true. I felt stretched, I was so tired. I had that almost ringing feeling in my head that I knew was exhaustion, as well as that ghostly ache through my muscles, almost like they wanted to be stretched, but it was all too much effort. And no stretching would relieve it.

My stomach, though, was a tight knot of stress. I could only hope food would help.

Wasn't the first time I'd worked on short sleep though. And if I survived this, it likely wouldn't be the last.

"You and me both," Des said, yawning yet again. "This up before dawn shit is for the birds. I could do with another couple hours of shuteye."

"No time for that," Edmund said. "Not if we must try to return before nightfall."

"Wait," I said. "Let's not skip that temper my emotions crap. What the hell are you talking about?"

"He's worried about control," Des said, before Edmund could jump in.

Edmund didn't let him carry the conversation though.

"Indeed," Edmund said. "If this is a vampire capable of fascination, then its greatest aid is an unquiet mind."

"What do I care if it gets fixated on things?"

"He means that in the old sense," Des said. "As in entrancing magic. Hypnosis. Enchantment."

"Oh," I said. "And you think that if I'm angry—"

"Strong emotions are a gateway into your mind. The stronger the emotion, the wider the gate stands. You must get your anger in hand, as soon as possible. Your thirst for revenge, as well."

"Well, maybe if breakfast would show up."

There was a knock at the door.

———

I HAD TO GIVE THE USHER THIS — THEY DID ROOM SERVICE BREAKFAST right. More food than we could eat. They even included plenty of fresh fruit, along with the best cheese omelet I'd had in ages. And the bacon was crisped just right. The orange juice tasted fresh-squeezed, and had plenty of pulp.

They even had great coffee. Good enough that the long-dormant connoisseur inside me began to stir, and approve.

As we ate, the other two caught me up on what they'd been doing.

Edmund's night had not been fruitful. He'd reached out to a few more local contacts, only to find that none would take his calls.

No response at all.

He was more troubled by this than I was. Back with *Seekers*, plenty of folks chose not to talk once the cameras started rolling. Didn't want to look like a fool to posterity.

In this case, it seemed that nobody wanted to draw the attention of a vampire. Or undead. Whatever.

"No," Edmund said after finishing his laundry list of potential contacts who should have answered him, but didn't, "you don't understand. The only reason they would completely avoid me is—"

"Yeah, yeah," Des said. He sounded more awake now that he'd had a pot of coffee and six English muffins, slathered in raspberry jam. "They think you're going to die. They think we're all going to die.

And if they help, us, they're worried that they'll go down with the ship."

"You want out?" I said, voice quiet, but intent. It was a question I stopped a piece of buttered sourdough toast on its path to my mouth to ask. I just didn't like the direction this conversation was going.

"You would offer me that? After I am the one who dragged you, all but literally kicking and screaming, into this fight?"

"The vampire brought the fight to me years ago. All you did was remind me. And yeah, if you want to get out and save what years you have remaining, I wouldn't blame you."

I looked over at Des. "Same goes for you. I appreciate the help, but this isn't your fight."

Des snickered, smirking a half-grin. "You'd go it alone? Even though you have no idea what you're up against?"

"I'll figure it out, or die trying. Least I can do for my friends."

"Why would you tell us to leave then?" Edmund said, his face set in a curious expression. "If you wish your revenge, or perhaps a reckoning, why would you not beg all the aid you could get?"

"Look," I said, dropping the toast and standing up. Agitation got me gesturing as I spoke. "Me? I have to do this. You guys don't. And I don't want anyone along who would rather be doing something else."

I shook my head. "If I'm going to die, I'll die doing what I know is right. If you help me and you die, I want you dying with that same feeling. I don't want you dying thinking that you shouldn't be there, or that you'd rather be somewhere else, or that..."

I kind of ran out of steam there. Threw my hands in the air. Dropped back down into my seat.

Des and Edmund, though, were still watching me. So I made myself finish my thought.

"Or that this isn't worth dying for."

"Finished?" Edmund asked.

I nodded.

"Excellent. Thank you for asking that."

"You want to leave?"

"We were both good enough to let you finish your thought, Sel. Now you must be good enough to allow us to reply."

I nodded. Made a go-ahead gesture.

"Thank you for asking that. I do not wish to see your mind distracted as we do what we must do, and I do not wish you to have doubts about either Des or myself."

Edmund placed one hand reverently on his chest. Bowed his head.

"The good Lord has graced me with many years on this earth, and I have always tried to work His will as I understood it. I help those in need of help, and I stop what evil I can stop."

He broke into a smile. A wide, honest smile. And then continued.

"That you would offer us the chance to leave this venture only affirms for me that aiding you is the right course of action. Assisting in revenge, I do not care for. But removing from the face of this earth a creature of evil that preys on the living, *that* is a just cause, and one I am more than happy to support. Even unto my own death."

"And as for me," Des said. He shrugged. "Wouldn't be here if I didn't want to go against a vampire. Isn't the first for me. With any luck, it won't be my last either."

He nodded over toward Edmund.

"And like Eddie here, I've lived longer than I ever figured to. Maybe longer than I should have, but that's not for me to say." He shrugged again. "Anyway, I'm in this to the end, for good or bad."

They both looked at me then. As though I should have had something important to say. Something meaningful. Some kind of big speech, like maybe the Saint Crispin's Day speech from *Henry V*.

But this wasn't exactly the Battle of Agincourt.

And I wasn't all that sure we were the happy few.

IT WASN'T UNTIL WE STEPPED OUT OF THE GLASS DOORS OF THE HOTEL and into the thick warmth of a Missouri summer morning that I wondered how we were going to get a cabbie — much less a limo driver — to be willing to go out the backroads and trails we'd need to drive to get where we were going.

Turned out, the answer was right in front of my face.

Parked at the curb, the doors open and the engine running, was a big, black Range Rover SUV. Four wheel drive. Plenty of space for the three of us, and any football teams we decided we might need to bring.

And a valet was handing gesturing for Edmund to enter the open passenger side.

"What the... How did..." I finally forced a full sentence out. "When the heck did you rent a car?"

"I ordered it online," Edmund said, as though it were the most obvious thing in the world. "Don't tell me you do not use a smartphone."

Des started laughing.

I bit down on my three initial replies. Gritted my teeth so hard that Des was still laughing as he hopped into the backseat.

Which meant I was driving. But then, I was the only one who knew anything at all about where we were going.

Still, I made them pay for springing this on me as a surprise. I took way more time than I needed to when I adjusted the seat, and the rearview mirror, and then the side mirrors, and then the rearview mirror again.

And then I looked at the temperature controls.

"If I might remind you," Edmund said, voice casual, but one eyebrow raised, "you were the one with a time limit on his daily activities. Not us."

"Fine," I said, and put the big thing in gear.

One touch and it lurched away from the curb much faster than I expected.

"Whoa!" I said, yanking off my foot.

"Mind the torque," Des said. "Not used to anything this big?"

"My little car has four cylinders, and it's a good day when they're all firing."

"Well, this beast has twice that," Des said through a chuckle. "So I suggest you get used to it while you still have pavement."

I sighed, and resolved to do just that. Focusing on the vehicle — as well as my awareness of *other* vehicles while driving an unfamiliar car — took me all the way to my first mile on the freeway before I felt comfortable enough to speak again.

"So," I said. "I hope you guys realize I only half remember where we're going. At best."

"Get us in the right direction," Edmund said, pulling his pendulum out of his jacket's inside pocket. "I will navigate from there."

"Where to first?" Des asked. "Cemetery or old lady hunting?"

"Cemetery," Edmund said. "I may be able to read vibrations that will aid in further remote viewing attempts."

"Eddie here hates it when he draws a blank," Des confided in me.

Edmund sighed.

"Sorry. I mean *Edmund* here hates it et cetera."

I shook my head and watched the road.

Not much traffic, at just about dawn. Mostly the long haul types, and the either early-risers or late-to-bed-ers. But at least the freeways were in good shape, and the big SUV glided along so smoothly I wondered if I needed to trade up from my little economy sedan.

As I drove, Des regaled us with his own research. Which mostly involved hitting the "right kind" of lowlife bars, where the lowlifes weren't all human, and information could be bought for a beer or a timely punch.

Mostly what he found out was that everyone local and not human had been glad the vampire was gone.

And they were all kinds of pissed that it was back.

Not much more information than that. But it was enough for me.

Well, no. Check that. Apparently Des had gotten a little information about the kind of vampire. Or at least, a rougher sense of where, in Europe, the creature seemed to come from. Because he and Edmund went back and forth about principalities and troop movements, with both of them knowing what war they were talking about, while I had no idea.

I didn't even know who was fighting.

"Guys," I said. "Any translations for the history impaired?"

"Difficult," Edmund said, watching his pendulum.

He was managing to keep it still. In a moving car. That was no easy feat. He had one elbow balanced on the armrest, yes, but the little chunk of wood should still have been swaying. At least when I changed lanes.

A honking horn brought my attention back to the road.

"Don't worry about the pendulum," Edmund said. "That's my responsibility. You only worry about driving."

"Did you hear anything Edmund was saying about your translation?"

I shook my head. I noticed a clean white sedan in my rearview mirror.

Was this the first time I'd seen it? I didn't think it was.

There'd been a clean white sedan behind us just after I pulled out of the hotel parking lot. And then again when we got on the freeway.

Clean white sedans weren't all that common though. And the three I'd seen back there were all midline Toyotas.

"You didn't catch what I was saying either, did you?" Des chuckled. "Don't worry about the Camry. I've been keeping an eye on it."

"Perhaps a condensed version of events will suffice for Sel, while keeping his attention on the road."

"Probably best," Des agreed. "Look. It's like this. Go back a few hundred years, and we didn't have nations quite the way we do today. There were city states in some places, competing would-be countries in others, a handful of empires ruling over most of them. And all told, a lot of places that only existed for a handful of years. At the *most*."

Des stopped talking until I looked at him in the rearview mirror.

"With me so far?" he asked.

"Lots of short term places. And you guys think this vampire might be from one of them?"

"Indeed," Edmund said. "From what Des determined, the creature appears to have characteristics from ... well, from what you would think of as western Romania. But also one or two qualities that appear to be of Russian origin."

"Possibly Austro-Hungarian — technically from a small province that held independence from the Holy Roman Empire for a time — instead of Russian," Des said. "Tough to say until we know more. Has to do with how it'll react to symbols of faith."

"Among other things," Edmund added.

"I don't think any of us is packing a cross," I said, "and I haven't been to church in years. What difference does it make about holy symbols."

"Actually," Edmund said, "we referred to symbols of faith, as opposed to symbols of a specific religion."

"What's the difference?"

"I could give you a cross, but obviously it would not avail you. You have not, as you said, attended a church service in several years. In fact, I think it likely that, should you hold a cross, your feelings would be mixed at best."

"That's one way to put it," Des said.

"What matters in that regard," Edmund said, speaking over whatever Des might have added, "is that you would be a poor representative of your chosen religion. As you have, for all practical spiritual purposes, little to no religion."

"I don't know that I'd go that far." I was surprised how offended I sounded. And felt. "I prayed just last night. And the night before."

"Did twenty-four robbers come knocking at your door?" Des asked.

I opened my mouth for a hot rejoinder to that, when I realized we were reaching our exit. I settled for a sharp breath and a little extra jerk of the wheel as I pulled off.

"Faith," Edmund said, as though Des hadn't spoken, "is a different matter. Most people, whether they admit it or not, do have faith in a higher power of some sort. And such people, likely including yourself, Sel, possess one or more objects that represent their faith—"

"Gas station," Des said. "Pull in now!"

Something about his tone had me jerking the wheel again, and braking, before I even thought about it.

I barely got us into the little Rotten Carl's. Wasn't a brand of gasoline I knew. And to be honest, with a name like that, it wasn't a brand I'd trust either. But then, we had a full tank of gas.

I was just about to ask why we pulled in, but I realized Des was watching the road.

Specifically, he was watching a clean, white Toyota Camry, drive past the gas station.

"Go, go, go!" Des said. "Follow it."

"Really," Edmund said, "I don't think there's any need for—"

"Go *now!*" Des said.

And it was that tone again. Wasn't just a barked order. Wasn't especially deep, and it didn't sound especially commanding.

But I obeyed as though the order were my own idea.

"What the fuck did you do to me?" I asked as I pulled back onto the road.

"Later," Des said, leaning forward. All his attention on the Camry. "Follow it."

"But—"

"Perhaps it is best to do as he bids," Edmund said. "Des' resources ... are not mine. I do not understand how his work. But when he is urgent, he is right more often than he is wrong."

"Gee, thanks for such a ringing endorsement," Des said. "Now, keep on it."

I focused on following the Camry. Kept us back a ways, at first. But Des thumped me on the shoulder.

"Fuck subtlety," he said. "They know they were following us, so they know we're following them."

"And if they're not?" I asked. "This could be coincidence."

Des snorted, but didn't say anything.

I shrugged and closed the gap at ramming speed.

I could see the driver now. Big looking guy. His head almost reached the roof of his car. Broad shoulders too. Sunglasses. And a ... black suit...

Black suit? In this heat?

What was this guy? Another Edmund?

I didn't ram the guy. But I saw him look at me in the rearview mirror.

No. I couldn't have. I couldn't see his eyes.

I would have sworn I saw him look at me in the rearview mirror. But I must have *felt* him do it. Because his head didn't move. And I couldn't see his eyes, not past those dark sunglasses.

But I was sure he met my eyes for a split-second.

And as soon as I he did, I hit the brakes. Kept us back about half a car-length.

The man in the black suit pulled over by the side of the road.

And it was a *side* of the road. Raw dirt off the edge of the asphalt.

We were between two farms, neither of which appeared to be growing summertime crops. Even though I could see furrowed rows for seeds, past the chicken wire fence.

Didn't make sense to me. But then, I was never exactly a farm boy.

No houses nearby. Not within at least four or five hundred yards. Not even any barns very close. Just two big stretches of plowed fields. And a smell in the morning air that made me think they'd either just fertilized, or there were cows somewhere nearby.

The sky was clear overhead. The sun still low, and yellow.

"Now what?" I said, as I pulled the SUV to a halt, three car lengths behind the white Camry.

"We get out," Des said.

I whipped off my seatbelt, opened my door, and hopped out before I noticed that Edmund had not moved, except to put away his pendulum.

"Coming?" I asked.

"I think not," Edmund said. "I shall leave this to you two gentlemen."

Dry dirt underneath me. Apparently none of those sudden

summer storms I remembered had hit around here. Though I was definitely keeping an eye open for them.

No traffic pulling past now either. We were a good quarter mile down the road from that gas station, and it seemed that only locals and idiots hunting vampires went any farther down this particular exit.

And no locals on the road right now.

Well, not in cars, anyway. Now that I was out — and had closed my door behind me — I could hear human sounds in the distance. A heavy engine — tractor maybe — and a loud whirring hum that had to be some other kind of farm equipment. Distant shouts too.

All of it hundreds of yards away. At least.

Which made me wonder just what we'd do if this guy pulled out a gun.

Des hopped out behind me, clapped me on the shoulder, and started toward the Camry.

The driver of the Camry got out.

Yes. This was a big guy. And I mean by my standards.

Well, he wasn't as big as Tangi. But few were.

He stood a little taller than me, and he was just as broad. His suit, now that I could get a good look at it, wasn't nearly as nice as Edmund's. Wasn't silk, and it wasn't cut right. Did nothing to show off the guy's frame. And as many muscles as I suspected he had, he should have been showing them off.

No tie either. That just looked gauche. And his shirt hadn't been dry cleaned for a time. Yellowed stains here and there.

Then I noticed his shoes.

While Edmund's shoes were perfectly shined, this guy's looked as though he'd been running through mud maybe twenty minutes ago. And he hadn't done more to clean them than run them under a hose. If that.

He didn't stand right either. No macho man stance. No simple standing-there stance. No, he had one foot forward just a little. Arms hanging at his sides, but slightly bent. Almost like it was a wrestling pose.

But his head was ducked forward too. Not quite a hunch. But close.

I could feel him look at me again. And my stomach tried to drop straight through the ground.

"Des," I whispered, "there's something off here."

"Too right there's something off," Des said aloud. "It's this prick right here."

He pointed at the man in the black suit.

"What is your problem, Desd—"

"Des is fine," Des said. "Not that we're on a first name basis."

Hearing the man in black speak was kind of like looking at him standing there. Off. His voice wasn't especially rough or especially smooth. He wasn't making his words a threat, and he wasn't apologizing.

It was more like ... more like the words, and the look, were just an act...

"What is he?" I whispered.

"Good for you, kid," Des muttered. Then louder, he added, "My boy here is a ghoul. A real western cemetery haunter. Aren't you?"

The man in black snarled, and it showed way too many big, yellowish teeth.

Teeth that looked like what they wanted most in this world was to rip my throat apart.

"Ghoul?" I managed in a small voice. Just how many monsters were real?

I was starting to think the answer was "all of them."

"Ghoul," Des said. "Which does beg the question. What the fuck are you doing tailing us? Don't know if you've noticed, but we're alive."

The ghoul kept snarling. Or maybe it was grinning. Tough to tell. I knew there were a lot of big, strong, ugly teeth involved.

I opened my mouth to ask a question, not even sure what question I'd ask, but Des spoke.

"See, kid, ghouls like to dine on the dead. Human dead, especially." That got the ghoul to lick its lips as Des kept talking. "Which means this one here better tell me why it's following us. You carrying a message from a bigger, badder threat? That it, ghoul boy?"

It shook its head slowly.

"Well," Des said, "you have five seconds to make with the words — in English — or I'm going to come over there and rip the head right off your twisted body. Got me?"

"You," it said. "Transmaniacon."

It pronounced that word better than I did. Kind of pissed me off, which meant I must have been less scared now. Maybe that was Des' confidence.

"Duh," Des said. "And?"

"Where the Transmaniacon goes, bodies follow."

"That's not—"

"Altamont," it said, then slowly rubbed its belly, a look of obscene pleasure on its face.

Des shook his head. "Well, as long as—"

"Never eaten Transmaniacon," the ghoul said. "Want to taste."

"Come try it."

"I wait. You seek the *hrrespaka*. I dine on what remains."

Hrrespaka? The vampire?

"Fuck that," Des said.

Des sprang forward.

The ghoul sprang to meet him.

And it looked less like a man now.

Instead of normal looking fingers, it had long, claw-like nails. Yellowish, brown and purple. It looked less ... solid too. Not in the incorporeal sense, but just ... thinner.

The two met in the air. Both wrapped their hands around each other's throats.

I opened the SUV's driver door, and popped the back.

I could hear the wrestling on the ground, and I hustled to the back of the vehicle while they fought.

The hatchback was open when I got there. I pulled up the carpeting. Yanked the tire iron out of the flat tire kit.

Then I turned on my old forty-yard sprint speed back to the fight.

The ghoul was on top of Des, and Des' face was going past red to purple. He still had his hands around the ghoul's throat, but it didn't seem to be helping him any.

Using every bit of my sprint as a wind-up, I did my level best to brain the ghoul.

Its skull made a satisfying crack when I hit it.

Des immediately reversed their positions. He reached out and took the tire iron from my outstretched hand.

The ghoul was still fighting, but had definitely weakened.

Worse, its sunglasses came off, and I saw its eyes.

Or, rather, I saw where its eyes should have been. Once *had* been. Now, only holes remained.

The thing could see. I would have sworn it could see. It was even driving a car.

But where its eyes should have been, only ragged, blackened empty holes that had once held eyes.

I turned and retched on the side of the road.

———

DES CAME UP TO ME A COUPLE OF MINUTES LATER, AFTER I HAD DUMPED out pretty much everything I'd eaten for breakfast. I was weak, and shaky, and sweating that kind of sickly sweat that I always hated. I associated it with food poisoning, and a bad night my sophomore year of college.

"It's all right," Des said in a soothing voice. "Natural reaction. Never seen a ghoul before, have you?"

I shook my head.

"The eye thing is rough. Even made me throw up, first time I saw it. Best way to kill 'em though. Straight in fatal path. Not to say it's easy. Have to be strong enough to break through the—"

"Could you not?" I asked, as bile tried to come up for one more round. Fortunately, I didn't have much bile left inside me either.

"Sorry," Des said, and offered me a pint bottle of water.

I was so grateful, I didn't even ask where he'd gotten it. If we'd brought supplies, I hadn't seen them.

Downing about half that bottle made me feel better. My stomach even felt like it might be on speaking terms with me before the end of the millennium.

And spitting out a few mouthfuls helped my tongue feel more generally positive about life.

I started to turn back toward the car, but Des stopped me with a hand on my shoulder.

"If you're still at all queasy, you don't want to see what's left of that thing."

I nodded, and turned back toward the farmland to stand up.

I couldn't stop myself from asking the question though. Too many years seeking out just this kind of thing — well, maybe not *exactly* this kind of thing — made me too curious by nature.

"Why don't I want to look?"

"Ghouls liquefy when they die. Not smelly, fortunately, but I doubt you want to see it."

I took his word for that. Instead I handed him my phone. Made him use the camera to capture a picture of it for later. When I wasn't quite on the hair-trigger of more vomit.

Des guided me back to the car, and into the back seat.

"But—" I started, but Des shook his head.

"I'll drive. And Edmund will navigate, via pendulum. You get some rest."

"But you didn't sleep any better—"

"One, I still have the benefit of breakfast in my system. You don't. Two, and maybe you're not going to want to hear this, but killing a ghoul is ... an energizing experience for me."

"Wait," I said, one foot already in the back of the car.

Des turned back to me. I realized I couldn't even see claw marks on his throat. I couldn't see a single sign that Des had just been through a fight for his life.

I wanted to ask about that, but I knew the answer would be "the knowledge beyond madness." So I asked another question instead.

"It knew the Transmaniacon Motor Club. And Altamont. What happened in Altamont?"

Des snorted and shook his head. "If you've never heard what happened in Altamont, you're younger than I thought."

I stared, waiting for him to get to the point.

"Long story short," he said with a sigh. "Big concert. My boys were there. A guy got killed. Nothing to do with us, but we were there."

"If it's nothing to do with you, why—"

"Ghouls were there too."

"But—"

"All right," Des said, and I heard actual anger in his voice for the first time. "That death, it wasn't an accident and it wasn't a casual murder either. It was a ritual sacrifice. Not us. We didn't do it. But ... let's just say it was a rival club. It was a big deal. Big enough we couldn't keep it quiet, like we like."

He shook his head, then continued in a softer voice. "Did a pretty good job of covering most of it up. Couldn't hide the one death though. News went nuts with it."

"If there were corpses and ghouls—"

"The ghouls," Edmund said, loudly, "were not allowed to feed on the sacrifice. That night is the source of a great many ills that befall California even unto today."

Des nodded.

"Now," Edmund said, "if we could continue? I should like to see this cemetery before we must stop for lunch."

I got into the back then.

There was a cooler on the floor, behind the driver's seat. Bottles of water and beer. An unlabeled brown bottle. Sandwiches. Crackers. Cookies.

No ice, but it was all cold.

I shook my head. Opened some crackers and another bottle of water, and settled in as we drove.

Edmund spoke out directions now, following the directions of his pendulum. We continued down that main road for a little ways, then turned off onto a side road I definitely didn't recognize.

There were hanging trees, kind of like willows, and this was a bumpy excuse for a dirt road. Hardly anything that had been smoothed at all, much less anything that ever hoped to see asphalt.

The trees closed in tight on either side of the vehicle. If we went much farther, I wasn't sure we'd be able to turn back. As it was, we might need to back up.

"Wrong turn," I said. "I don't know any of this."

"It must be more direct," Edmund said. "I feel only certainty through pendulum, and I should be able to recognize the vibrations of the cemetery, as many times as I have remote viewed it."

I shut up, then, and let them handle the driving.

We didn't pass anything I recognized. We didn't pass anything I thought *anyone* would recognize. There were no buildings at all along the way. No signs of human life, except periodic Keep Out signs posted on a tree here and there.

Apparently the woods on either side of the road were private property.

Which made me wonder about the road we were on. But no one seemed interested in stopping us, so I didn't bother asking.

And sure enough, only about ninety minutes later, we were stopping in front of a place I never thought I'd see again in my lifetime.

A place I never thought I'd *want* to see again.

That little goddamn cemetery.

9

Even from inside the big SUV, the cemetery looked as though nature had tried to erase it. Just wipe out all evidence that it had ever existed.

More than a bit overgrown with grasses now. I could hardly pick out where the grave stakes were, if any of them were still standing.

I forced myself to turn from it for a moment. I needed to get out of the car, and use the muggy morning heat as a reminder that I was still alive.

My heart was pounding fast. Just meant I was still alive.

Sweat broke out on my brow. Meant I was still alive.

I could hear my blood rushing past my ears. I could feel twitches of tension all through my body. My groin clenched like it was thinking of trying to hide inside me.

All of these, just more signs that I was alive. I was back *here*, but I was alive.

I had to focus on that. Had to focus on what I could see. Hear. Smell. What I knew. Focus on now. Not on then.

I had to learn things here, or this whole trip would have been for nothing.

I knew all that. Still even after a full minute of sitting there, I was still in the backseat.

Des and Edmund didn't wait for me. They got out just as soon as Des killed the engine.

I was the only one still sitting. Still locked behind my door. Strapped into the leather seat with a seatbelt.

Come on, Sel. Get out.

Had to force myself to take off the seatbelt. Paid strict attention to the little details. The feel of my shoulder as my arm pulled across my body to the seatbelt. The cool press of plastic under my thumb as I triggered the release.

The soft whir of the seatbelt retracting. The pressure on my hand until I released the catch. Let it fly back to its post at my shoulder.

Each step was closer to where I needed to be. What I needed to do.

My hand found the door handle. Opened it.

Good. There was that muggy warmth I was waiting for.

Immediately I smelled life. That helped too. Wildlife. Growth. Those strange Missouri backroads smells I could only associate with green, growing things. No idea if I was smelling the grasses or the flowers or the trees, or all of them at once.

Todd had known. Could have told me. I never bothered to ask.

Shouldn't have thought of Todd.

I could almost feel that night in my head. The hours of driving on those backroads. Todd yelling. Page's fury at the network heads for sending us out here. Tangi telling me little jokes. Offering me the Twinkie of Peace.

The relief of finally getting here, after the bust that was those stupid crossroads.

Even the release of urinating off the side of the road, beside the van.

That was *then*. This was *today*.

Des and Edmund needed me here *today*. Todd, Page and Tangi needed me here *today*.

They all needed me to get my shit together, so we could take this monster down once and for all.

I got out of the SUV. Shut the door without slamming it.

And the first thing I did was look up.

A smear of white clouds in the sky. Odd feeling in the air, that I didn't think was just the mugginess. Sign of a coming flash storm maybe?

Maybe.

I wasn't ready to turn back to the cemetery yet. Looked down next.

The road we were on was worse than I remembered, from years of rain and disuse. Or maybe disrespect.

I wondered how often people came this way. Whether they were hunters, or something else. Maybe local kids came through here to scare each other and make out. Maybe...

Wondering that gave me a moment's space in my head. Made me realize something else.

I could hear birds.

Birds. Birds were singing. Or at least chirping.

"Birds," I said. My eyes still on the ground.

I raised my voice. "Last time, there was no wildlife near here. But I hear birds."

But that reminded me of something.

I turned to Edmund. Clasped him by the sleeve. Got a surprised look in those gray eyes, but I had his attention.

"No. There was *one* bird. A night bird of some kind. Gave a single cry when we arrived that night."

"Shapeshifting?" Des said, his face set in a grimace that suggested he doubted shapeshifting was the answer.

"Why not?" I started to say, but Edmund shook his head.

"There may be vampires that truly take other forms, but none I have heard of." He glanced at Des, then back at me. "I suspect you triggered a guardian. That might have been what called the vampire to return."

"But ... this was its home?"

"Possibly. It may only have been an anchor." Edmund grimaced. "Too many variables to be certain yet."

"But you called it a vampire."

"And so it must be, or the ghoul would never have risked its wrath."

"Kind of a symbiotic relationship there," Des said. "Vamps drain, and the ghouls get leftovers. Neat and tidy."

I couldn't believe it, but I laughed. I don't know if it was the absurdity of the mental image, or my situation, or just the tone of Des' voice, but I laughed.

And that laughter, that made me feel better. Got some of the clenched knots in my shoulders, arms and legs to ease up a little. I even rolled my neck and shoulders around.

Made me remember something else, too.

"What's a *hrrespaka*?"

"A—" Des started, but Edmund interrupted him.

"*Hrrespaka?* Or *hrrespakut?*"

"The first one, I think," I said.

Des nodded. "Both just mean vampire, don't they? I don't exactly speak ghoul."

"Nor do I," Edmund said, "but I have read *Cultes des Goules*. *Hrrespaka* and *hrrespakut* refer to different varieties of vampire."

Edmund gave me that searching look of his. "You're certain it was the former? *Hrrespaka?*"

His pronunciation was sharper than mine. Rolled his r's a little more.

I nodded. "Definitely didn't hear a 't' on the end, anyway."

"That would explain why the local community displays such anger at the creature returning. The *Hrrespaka* is a corrupter. Its presence in an area ... fouls a community."

"That rules out the Norwegian breeds," Des said. "Not sure about Russian."

"It's neither," Edmund said, with a grimace. "The ... western Romanian elements remain in play. The rest though ... betrays a *starry* influence."

Des snapped a glare at Edmund. "You're sure?"

Edmund nodded.

"And I'm the only one of us around here," Des grumbled.

"Do I get to find out what that means?" I asked.

"Hope you never do," Des said.

"The three of us will have to suffice." Edmund put his hand on my shoulder. Showed me some sympathy in his gray eyes. "I'm sorry, Sel. I would spare you this if I could. But we will need your assessment of the cemetery, as well as our own."

I sighed. And nodded.

Finally, I turned to face the scene of the crime.

The trees behind the cemetery had crept closer since that night. Sent up shoots that had grown into smaller trees right behind what little remained of that old fence.

Just a few fence posts left now. All of them raw wood, and all of them rounded, which now made me wonder if the vampire had done that. Made them less useful as potential weapons.

Assuming they were the right kind of wood in the first place.

Since apparently that mattered.

I almost asked if the *hrrespaka* angle told us what kind of wood we needed. But that could wait. Asking now, that was just another way for me to delay what I needed to do.

I needed to understand what was here now. Contrast it with what was here before. The differences, the details, they might be crucial to our efforts.

No flowers still growing around the outside of that fence line. Some of those yellow ones still grew close by. Primroses or Black-Eyed ... somethings. Todd would have known what kind. Whatever they were, one kind had clearly choked out the other, and the ones that remained no longer grew in anything that could even pretend to be a neat row, or associated with the cemetery.

Seemed to be there more by happenstance than design.

As for the old graves, from where I stood, they looked overgrown with thick wild grass.

My heart was pounding hard enough now that I could feel it in my throat. My ears could barely hear those birds chirping-singing over the sound of my own rushing blood.

I felt flushed. All the way up my face. My ears burned.

But I made my feet start moving.

One step. Then another. I kept my eyes on that thick wild grass. On those fifteen graves. Or maybe eighteen. Whichever.

Didn't really matter now, I supposed.

I could feel the cushioning of wild grass under my feet now. The hot, muggy air sliding around me like I was walking through invisible fog.

But I made it past the fence line.

Didn't waste time with the other graves. I went straight to the back right corner.

Where no grass grew at all.

Eight years since I'd last been here. And still, nothing there but withered, gnarled, crispy-looking bits of yellow among a few shards of glass. Grass that had never gotten higher than an inch before it died a horrible death, leaving only its corpse behind. Hardly covering the dead dirt beneath.

And that dirt looked dead too.

I crouched down. Moved some of the wild grass beside me.

Sure enough, the soil there looked rich and dark.

The dirt where the vampire's grave had been looked pale. Dry.

"How?" I asked. "How could it still be like this? How could the rest of the cemetery be so overgrown, but here, just ... nothing?"

"The creature is a *hrrespaka*," Edmund said from behind me. "A corrupter. It corrupts all that it touches, and clearly, it remained here for some time."

"Will the land ever recover?"

"Perhaps," Edmund said. "If we slay the cause."

Des stepped up beside me now.

"All right if I approach?" he asked in a soft tone.

I nodded. Then waved my hand over my shoulder for Edmund to come up too.

"The glass shards," Des said as Edmund came closer. "Those look familiar or different?"

"Broken mason jars," I said. "Hard to be sure. These aren't as intact as they were the last time. But it looks like the same number of jars. Mostly blueish, but also some clear."

"You are certain?" Edmund said, crouching beside me with more grace than I expected. He moved well for an old man. "You have no doubts?"

"Of course I have doubts," I said, shaking my head. "I haven't been here in eight years, and I barely paid attention to them then. That was Page's thing. Her proof of the folk magic."

"Shame the oils and such dried out," Des said. "Coulda been useful."

"What remains will suffice." Edmund pulled a handkerchief out of his jacket pocket and picked up a large shard of blue glass. He studied it closely.

"Yes," he said. "I would say this once held more oil. I can detect hints of its residue."

"Smell?" Des asked.

"None that remains, I fear."

"Can you do something with that?" I asked.

"Of course," he said. "I can track the conjure man or woman who assembled the charm."

"Pendulum," Des said, winking at me.

I felt a bit chagrined. Had to start thinking in broader terms than I was used to. To try to see the world more the way that Todd and Page did. Broader terms than them, even, if I could do it.

But I had to start somewhere.

"What about the vibes of this place?" I asked. "Getting anything?"

"I will check once the two of you withdraw. First, though, I must know what else we can determine with our more usual senses."

"Well, everything about this place has grown, except here." I pointed to the dead grave. "And that no new mason jars have shown up indicates the vampire's been gone quite a while."

"*Hrrespaka,*" Edmund corrected me.

"I'd just as soon stick with vampire, if you don't mind."

"Why?" Des asked, and the question sounded important.

I had to think about it. I supposed it would be good for me to get more precise with my language, if I was going to do this.

But I wasn't going to do this.

I mean, I *was*. I was going to hunt and kill this particular *hrrespaka*, but I wasn't going to make a habit of chasing down the things that went bump in the night.

This was about Todd, Page and Tangi.

And that night, we weren't hunting a *hrrespaka*. Didn't even know what one was.

We were hunting a vampire.

And that was what I was going to call this thing until it was no more.

I tried to convey that. Tried to put it into words. But I was never the on-air talent type. Des either understood quickly or got bored, because he moved around to continue his own inspection.

After six or seven more abortive attempts, Edmund finally put it better than I ever could have.

"The creature haunting your life is a vampire. To call it anything else might divest it of your connection."

I nodded.

"Very well," Edmund said. "Let us all do likewise then. But I do ask that you remember — in the future — that the specific breed of vampire was known as a *hrrespaka*."

"Fine," I said.

"All right," Des said, ambling back over. "While you boys have been playing vocabulary games, I've figured out pretty much every-thing I can figure out about this place."

"And?" I asked.

"There was a vampire here. There isn't one now."

"Very good," I said, not hiding the sarcasm.

"Let me finish," he said. "And I know what it feels like now, so I'll know it when we find it."

"I'll never forget what it looked like."

"Good for you," Des said. "But now if it kills you before you can finger it, I'll still be able to recognize it. Even if it changes its look."

"The *hrrespaka*," Edmund started, then stopped himself. "This particular variety of vampire has no power to change its appearance. Even unto the clothes it wore."

"But..." I frowned. "But that thing, it was dressed like an American. It can't be as old as you said. Not if even its clothes don't change."

"Odd," Edmund said, then joined me in my frown. "You are quite right. I can recall its features, and though the core of its appearance might have been blended from European stock, its mannerisms and mode of dress were distinctly American."

"Wasn't finished," Des said, waving a hand.

Edmund gestured for Des to continue.

"There's more," he said. "The grave knows its vampire is back. There's a connection between them. Not a sentience, per se. Not in an absolute way. More like..."

Des frowned as he picked his next words. Took him long enough that I almost accused him of needing a vocabulary game himself. But then he started again.

"More like the vampire left a bit of itself behind when it left. Or maybe, that's how it corrupts. Spreads a bit of itself wherever it goes."

"And the portion that remains here," Edmund said. "You're certain it remains intact?"

"Positive," Des said with a nod. "In fact, I suspect it's already let daddy know we're here."

"Interesting," Edmund said. He began to stroke his chin as he considered the implications.

"Wait," I said, my eyes widening until my eyeballs almost popped out of my head. Which made me think of the ghoul, and then it was all I could do to get the rest of my words out in a rush, before I thougth *too much* about the ghoul.

"What if it can't die as long as any part of it remains?"

"Got that backwards," Des said. "Can't get rid of its corruption until we axe the source. Then all the little bits of it will die off too."

"Contagion," Edmund muttered.

"What?" I asked.

"Magical principle," Des said. "What was once connected is always connected."

"This particular variety of vampire appears to exist all but entirely through that principle." Edmund dropped his hand from his chin. Looked urgently from me to Des and back. "That must be how it is still connected to you. Though it implies I should not have lost my ability to remote view it. If I could—"

"Tick tock," Des said, tapping his wrist where a watch was not.

"Quite right," Edmund said. "And we've much to do today. If you could both wait beside the vehicle?"

I hot-footed it back to the SUV.

Part of my rush was to get away from the cemetery again. But I have to admit, some of it was that I was just eager to watch Edmund work.

EDMUND CLOSED HIS EYES. TILTED HIS FACE TOWARD THE HEAVENS.

He spread his arms wide.

I lost a moment reflecting on how unfair it was that I was sweating in this muggy heat, but Edmund seemed perfectly cool and at ease in a silk freaking suit.

Even Des was sweating. Though not as much as I was.

Edmund's lips moved, as though in prayer. If he said anything, I couldn't hear him over the singing birds though.

At least my heart had gotten back under control. I was getting a little worried about that. My muscles were still mainly on tension lockdown, but my breaths were getting deeper again, and my heart rate was almost normal.

My stomach even growled, which made Des elbow me. He was watching too.

Edmund spun slowly in place. Another graceful movement, which made me wonder if the man had dance training or something. He was standing in fancy shoes, in the middle of a ridiculously overgrown cemetery, but he spun in place with his eyes closed as though he were in the middle of a flat wooden stage.

He spun again. His arms moved up and down every so often. Not a regular kind of movement, but as though they were responding to something. As though he could feel something in the muggy air that made him move around it.

His head snapped down. His closed eyes focused on the dead grave.

He looked sharply left and right. Eyes still closed.

He spun again. Began walking swiftly through the cemetery. Stepping nimbly between the graves, his hands moving up or down every so often, even turning at the wrist as they did now.

He seemed to turn at random. Then he started tracing the limits of the cemetery. Walking it as though following a fence, even though hardly any fence remained. He occasionally stepped higher when he needed to step over something like a fallen fence post.

And all of this with his eyes closed.

Maybe he should have just pulled this trick in the restaurant. Would have impressed me more than telling me that my food would arrive hot.

And then, just as fast, Edmund seemed to finish.

He turned to face us. Opened his eyes.

But he wasn't smiling. In fact, the look in those gray eyes of his was urgent.

"We must move quickly. The creature has allies, and they're on their way."

10

———————

No time for questions.

Des had the keys, so Des hopped in the driver's seat. I jumped into the back, and Edmund was in the front passenger seat, affixing his seatbelt, even before I had my door closed.

Des started the engine.

"Onward or backward?" he asked Edmund.

"Onward," Edmund said, before I could get the word out.

What kind of question was that anyway?

Edmund answered that for me.

"They are coming from the freeway. We have a little time, but they've been moving for some time now. They could be on us soon. If we go back the way we came."

"Head-on collision," Des said. "And you boys might not survive that."

"What kind of allies could it have?" I asked.

"Ghouls," Des said.

"They are one option," Edmund said, and his voice sounded bitter. "That the fiend is a corrupter broadens the scope of possibilities. Even unto some of those I might have called friends."

"Cops," I said. "It gets us arrested, we have major problems when it comes for us."

"Shit," Des said. "Good point."

He pounded the accelerator. The SUV lurched way too fast down that bumpy dirt road. I slammed against my seatbelt every half-second or so.

"You're … going … to … trigger … the … air bags," I said, words shaky from all the jostling.

And that wasn't the worst part.

The worst part were the flashing red and blue lights.

They were in front of us, not behind us.

A cop SUV. Coming straight at us.

Des looked for all the world like he was going to ram it.

"Sel and I would not survive," Edmund said. "Or at the very least, I would not."

Des swore — and it was a word in a language I didn't recognize — and slammed on the brakes.

He wrestled with the steering wheel. Fought it and kept us, somehow, on that little dirt road and not, say, slamming into one of the many nearby oak trees.

The cop SUV pulled a fancy maneuver and skidded to a stop, sideways to us.

One of the cops jumped out, shotgun in hand.

The other got out of the driver's seat, hand on the butt of his pistol, but nothing drawn yet.

Both of the cops were young. Still on the south side of thirty. They were in decent shape, but both had pot bellies going. And they were both so pale white that they might have burned without their "smoky" hats.

Couldn't see the door of their car from where I sat.

"Are they local?" I asked. "They might be out of the jurisdiction."

"Won't matter," Des said. He had his hands on the steering wheel at the ten and two positions. Like he was expecting a regular traffic stop.

"Out of the car," The driving trooper, the lead trooper, said without coming any closer. "No sudden movements. Don't want to make my partner here any jumpier than he already is."

All three of us exaggerated our slow movements as we removed our seatbelts, then got out of the SUV. I had my hands in the air, but I was the only one.

"What seems to be the problem officer?" Edmund asked. "I realize we were going a trifle fast for conditions, but that would be my fault. I always loved speed in my youth, and I asked my oldest friend to indulge me one last time. To show my grandson here a touch of what his grandfather was like in his heyday."

"Hands on the hood," the lead cop said, and his attention was all on Des.

Mr. Shotgun, too. He was focused on Des.

Des assumed the position. I did too. Edmund said, "Must I, officer? With my arthritis—"

"Do it," the lead cop said.

"Certainly officer..."

"Jones," the lead cop said. "And this is my partner. Smith. Got it?"

I tried to spot a name tag. It was covered in black electrical tape. Not a good sign.

They weren't wearing their badges either.

Worse and worse.

"I suppose your dash cam..." I started, and Jones finished for me. "It's having trouble today. Body cams too. Damndest thing."

Smith snickered. An ugly sound.

Edmund put his hands on the side of the SUV.

Jones came over to Des. Started frisking him.

"Mind if you tell us what this was about, Officer *Jones*?" Des asked.

"Heard about some vandals in an SUV. Had to check it out, and we found us a Hell's Angel. Didn't we Smitty?"

"That's right, sir. A gen-yu-wine Hell's Angel."

"Where's your bike, boy?"

"You boys are supposed to be finding it right now," Des lied. "Reported it stolen last night. Or don't you guys go after actual criminals? Just find it more convenient to harass innocent private citizen, with your ... weapons?"

That got Des a thump on the head. Smacked his skull against the SUV.

"Hey!" I pulled my hands up.

"Stay there," Des said sharply.

"Do as he says, boy," Jones said to me. "Or maybe we'll take a closer look at you too."

"Don't think we need to," Smith said, and I could hear the telltale sound of recognition in his voice. "Ain't that the vampire kid?"

Jones looked over at me.

Physically, I'd aged a bit in the last eight years. It was true. But my overall look was much the same.

And I'd made the mistake of wearing a *Seekers* tee shirt.

"Yes. It. Is," Jones said, giving me an ugly smile. "You back here looking for your vampire, boy? Who you gonna shoot this time?"

"Gotta be careful about that," Smith added, with an evil grin of his own. "Some things out here, they shoot back at know-nothing Hollyweird types."

"Guys," I said. "You're mistaking me for someone else. I'm just a fan of the show." I sighed. "I admit, I wanted to see the grave that was supposed to hold a vampire. Famous, you know, in some internet circles. Took me years to piece together where to actually find it."

"Oh, yeah?" Jones said. "Get a good eyeful of bloodsucker did you?"

Both the cops were looking at me.

Which must have been why Des chose then to make his move.

He slammed Jones' head against the roof of the SUV hard enough to dent it. The roof, and maybe the guy's skull too.

Smith turned the shotgun on him, but Des was already holding the groggy Jones between himself and the shotgun.

And he'd grabbed the pistol out of Jones' holster. A 9mm of some type. Had it pointed at Smith.

"Now you just set that shotgun down on the dirt road, nice and easy," Des said. "Wouldn't want any accidents out here where there are no witnesses, and no backup anywhere near you."

"Backup's on its way, shitbird," Smith said. "First rule of pursuing the armed and dangerous. Always call for backup."

"And the second rule," Des said, "is that you lie about it when you haven't. Like, say, if you're going out of bounds, with your badges off, your nametags covered, and your body cams off."

Des shook his head. "You boys even real cops?"

"Pull the trigger and you'll find out how real we are," Smith said. "On duty or not. Wearing our badges or not. We don't like cop killers down here in Missouri. Especially not piece of shit Hell's Angels."

While they were talking, I slipped my hands down off the side of the SUV. Crouched down. Crept up around the front of the SUV. Got a good view of Smith, while they were still talking.

"So you put the gun and my partner down, shitbird, and maybe I won't have to kill all three of you."

"See," Des said, "things like that make me not want to play nice. You put the gun down, then all I'll do is blow out your tires. You won't be able to follow us, and this looks like a nice day for a *hike*."

That had to be my cue.

I poured on full speed and blitzed Smith just like I was back on the football field.

And tackling was always one of my best skills.

I slammed into Smith.

Smith's shotgun went off.

I think I heard his ribs crack when I drove my shoulder into him. I *know* he hit the ground so hard he lost anything like air. And when I followed the tackle with a right cross, Smith was officially down for the count.

I kicked away his shotgun. Whipped my head around to see what he shot.

He shot Jones. Or, rather, he shot Des' human shield. That just worked out to be the same thing. Looked like Jones had taken the brunt of the blast to his chest.

At pretty close range.

"Is he dead?" Edmund asked, worry in his voice, as he stepped around the SUV to join us.

"Not yet," Des said, wiping his prints off the pistol. "Will be soon."

"No," Edmund said. "We must save him."

That was all I needed to hear. I raced over to the cop car. Had to be a first aid kit in there.

Des and Edmund were still arguing when I got back.

"These guys came here to *kill* us," Des said. "Only one of them dies, they get off light."

"That does not make it right," Edmund said.

"They're allied with a *vampire*," Des said. "I think we left right and wrong behind."

I shook my head at that. Edmund didn't settle for a gesture.

"We do not know that they were willing allies. They might be innocent men, corrupted by the fiend and not in control of their own actions."

I settled the issue by ripping open Jones' shirt.

A BUMPY DIRT MISSOURI BACKROAD. TERRIBLE PLACE TO PERFORM meatball surgery. Especially since I was no surgeon.

And hot and muggy as it was, I suspected Jones might bleed out even faster than normal. Had to be bad conditions to have a wound like that.

Well, there were never *good* conditions to have a wound like that. But this place had to be a haven for infection.

And I only needed one look at Jones to know he was in bad shape.

Lots of blood. And no doubt he had plenty of shot in his chest. I wanted to help him, but...

"I can't get those things out," I said.

"Leave that part to me," Edmund said. "Prepare the antiseptic and bandages."

Edmund sat there in the middle of the dirt road. His eyes closed. Mumbling to himself.

He moved his hands above Jones' body. Jones' chest was barely moving. If we were going to save this guy, we needed to act fast.

Des dropped down to kneel behind Jones' head, swearing under his breath. He put his hands on Jones' temples. Began to mumble softly himself.

Jones' body began to shudder directly underneath Edmund's hands. Little mewling sounds of complaint made it past his lips.

But bits of shotgun shot began to make their way up out of his skin.

A wave of cold washed over me. Remote viewing was one thing. This was fucking *telekinesis*.

What else could Edmund do?

The shot wasn't moving fast, and it was only coming up directly underneath Edmund's hands, but it was coming up.

And Des, he was definitely doing something up there with Jones' temples. I couldn't tell if he was soothing the guy, or stabilizing him or what.

"Sel," Edmund said, his voice strained.

...and I just remembered I was supposed to do more than watch.

I dug out antiseptic, cotton pads, and gauze. Everywhere the shotgun shots came up out of Jones, I started cleaning the wounds as best I could.

Jones' shuddered harder when the cold antiseptic touched his skin. Des mumbled louder, though, and Jones seemed to settle.

Took us a while. I started half-expecting Smith to wake up and shoot us while we worked. But he seemed to be out for the count.

It was a slow process. But eventually Edmund seemed convinced we'd gotten all the lead out of Jones. By then I'd cleaned the wounds as well as I could. And as gently, because I was wary of causing more damage.

Des took charge of wrapping the bandages into place.

I sighed, sat back on my knees, and checked on Smith.

Smith sat up. Blinking. Grimacing. Holding his side with one hand, and rubbing his jaw with the other.

"What happened?" he asked. He sounded like he'd been out of it for days.

"Your buddy here took friendly fire," Des said.

Smith jumped to his feet.

Mistake. Too woozy. Started to fall right back down. I caught him by the shoulders. He still hissed pain and clutched his cracked or broken ribs.

"Easy there," I said, and took a chance. "They're gone. You are your partner were here chasing some bad guys. It went badly. They got away. You're lucky we happened along when we did. Your friend here might not have made it."

Smith looked at us. Blinked. Looked down at Jones. Blinked again.

"You should get him to a hospital as fast as is safe," Edmund said. "We've extracted the lead, but he should still be seen by a professional."

"A *current* professional," Des said, giving Edmund a sharp look. "I've let my creds slide. But I still remember my field medic training."

"Yeah," Smith said. "But—"

Took us only another minute or two to convince Smith, or whatever his name really was, that what mattered more than anything else was getting Jones back to a hospital ASAP. And himself, because I was starting to worry about his ribs.

Probably only took that long because Smith was woozy.

Soon, though, the three of us were back in the SUV, and on the road again.

Edmund looked wiped out. His skin was pasty, and he had more sweat on his forehead than I had ever seen before.

Just one line of beads, but that was still more sweat than I'd seen on *Edmund*.

"You all right?" Des said. "We need to head back?"

"I ... perhaps it is best."

"Lunch," I said. "He needs food. Maybe worse than I do."

My stomach rumbled loudly.

Des got us moving again.

LUNCH WAS DINER FOOD AT A GREASY SPOON ON THE SIDE OF THE nearest major freeway. The place was actually a knock-off of a major chain. Had the nerve to call itself Lennys.

Anyway, even just the thought of lunch did great things for me, and it did even better things for Edmund. He stopped sweating — though the AC might have helped — and sat up in his seat as we pulled into the parking lot. By the time we were seated in the vinyl booth, he looked less pasty, though not quite himself yet.

A good, thick burger — with extra grease — was just what my stomach ordered. Along with about a half-gallon of soda.

Des joined me and ordered the same, except that he had the French fries while I had the onion rings.

Edmund, of course, couldn't settle for anything so prosaic. Not with his palate.

To be honest, I think the only reason he accepted stopping there in the first place was that he hadn't been in shape to argue.

Or maybe it was the lack of reasonable alternatives.

Edmund had two slices of dry toast. Coffee. A bowl of fruit, and a small salmon salad.

I wasn't convinced that fish was a good thing to order in a place like this. Mentioned it to Des while Edmund went to clean up in the restroom.

"Trust me," Des said. "If Edmund's instincts tell him to eat the fish, he should eat the fish."

"Did you know he could do telekinesis?"

"No," Des said. "Not surprised though. Guy's like a Swiss army knife of psychic powers."

"Skills, if you please," Edmund said, rejoining us. "Either of you could learn to move things with your mind, had you the interest and discipline to train at it."

"How much training are we talking about?" I asked.

Edmund raised an eyebrow. "Did you see the amount of effort involved?"

I nodded.

"And did you notice how draining even that effort was?"

I nodded, then frowned.

"Indeed," Edmund said. "The training will not give you tricks to perform at parties. But, if the situation arises, you might be able to save a man's life. At some small cost to yourself."

"Either way," Des said, "there's no time to learn it now. If we live through this, then you can play psychic all you want."

Edmund frowned at that, but our lunch arrived, so he let it go.

We were all three hungry enough that we ate in silence, for a change.

By the time we were finished — and Edmund had managed to pay the bill without my noticing — I was just about to ask what was next.

That was the moment Des focused in tight on Edmund.

"How are you?" Des said. "Don't hold back, now. I'll know if you're lying."

Des seemed to emanate quiet. Which was weird because there were plenty of other diners making plenty of other noise.

But I couldn't shake the sense that there was some stillness in the air, the way Des focused on Edmund.

"I am fine," Edmund said.

"Lying," Des said.

"Very well," Edmund said. "I am tired. I do confess it. I would like nothing more than to return to our hotel suite and rest for a few hours."

"All right then," Des said, but Edmund held up a hand. Took a commanding air as he continued.

"But I shall do no such thing. Nor shall you try to make me."

"Edmund," Des started, but Edmund shook his head.

"We are pressed for time. Already the fiend moves against us, and is likely to do so again. It will know we foiled its first attempt."

"He does have a point there," I said.

I felt as though I should have felt worse about saying that. Edmund here, he was old enough to believably tell someone he was my grandfather. He should have had plenty of chance to rest when he needed it.

But this creature had to die. Edmund knew the risks when he agreed to stay on for this.

"Fine," Des said, shaking his head. "But realize this, both of you. If we're not at our best when the big fight comes, we're less likely to survive it."

"We need do only one more thing while the sun still shines," Edmund said.

Des and I both turned to Edmund.

He held up his large shard of blue glass, taken from the cemetery.

"We must trace the conjure person who constructed this fetish."

———

DES AND EDMUND ARGUED ABOUT THE DEFINITION OF A FETISH ON THE way out to the car. I managed to get the keys back, though, and made Des return to the backseat.

Seemed like the least I could do. Let him get a little rest.

Couldn't do much for Edmund though. He had to navigate.

Edmund, once he settled into his seat, pulled out his pendulum. Then he set the shard of blue glass on his lap, in the center of the handkerchief he'd wrapped it in.

And then I drove, following Edmund's directions.

It seemed that, with the shard of glass to follow, the pendulum could connect the vibration of whatever remained of the spell on the shard — and I had to accept that spells were real and that one had been put on that glass — and the person who cast that spell in the first place.

From there, it was a question of Edmund reading the pendulum's movement and interpreting it into driving directions.

Took us all of two hours, mostly more backroads, before we reached what had to be our destination. It wasn't quite mid-afternoon at this point.

The destination, well, it wasn't what I expected.

First of all, I'd expected it to be part of a community. A house in a suburb, or maybe even in a downtown urban area. I don't know why I figured that part, but it was what made sense to me.

But no, we were out in the middle of nowhere. West of Springfield — not east, like the cemetery — and just into the foothills of the Ozark mountain range.

Taller trees around here. Some variety of evergreen. Pine, maybe. Or spruce. Something like that. Not redwood or sequoia. I knew that much. But they had that vague, Christmassy smell.

Given Edmund's example, I figured anyone who was good at their "extranormal skills" had to be living it high on the hog.

But the shard of glass, it led us to a little shack of a place.

The walls looked like aluminum, painted pale blue, once upon a time. Paint needed primer to hold, though, and whoever painted this place forgot that step. It was chipped and peeling pretty much everywhere.

Didn't seem to bother the occupants, though. They just painted over it with occult symbols.

Oh, I didn't know what any of them meant. That was Page and Todd's thing. But I knew occult symbols when I saw them, and I was looking at them now. They had those kinds of arcs and curves, circles and angles and squiggles. Stuff that would have been at home on a heavy metal album cover.

And I think some of them combined to look like a representation of the Tree of Life, though I couldn't be sure about that.

The roof, it didn't have any symbols on it. It was soft tar, and it was in better shape than the paint.

Very good shape, in fact.

The front door was solid, and red, with some kind of swirly symbol painted in the center of it, in black.

I half expected to see animal bones lying at the doorstep, but there weren't any.

There were cats though. Living ones, I mean. Lots of cats around here. Sunning themselves, or prowling, or watching us.

The grass wasn't all that tall either. It was crabgrass, but it was neatly mown, and the hedge that grew on either side of the "house" was trimmed to a reasonable size. Almost as though there should have been neighbors past those hedges, instead of tree stumps, weeds, and wild grass.

The cats were already announcing our arrival, with their meowing.

Or maybe I was just getting into the spirit of looking for omens and signs.

"Looks like the right place," I said.

Des didn't say anything. Edmund said, softly, "It is definitely the source of this fetish. But it may be the wrong place, if you take my meaning."

"He means be careful," Des translated, "and don't say anything stupid."

"Yeah," I said, getting out of the car. "I was planning on doing *all* the talking. Maybe trying to go all good-cop-bad-cop third-degree. That was the plan."

I shook my head. But Des and Edmund got out of the car.

"You better take lead here," Des said quietly.

Edmund nodded.

Both of them looked way too uncertain for my taste.

I stopped them with a hand on each chest.

"What aren't you guys telling me?"

They looked at each other.

"Most conjure," Edmund said, "has strong roots in Christianity, one way or another. Catholicism for some, Protestantism for others. But most have connections to a Christian baseline, if you will."

"So?" I said. "Isn't that Tree of Life thing Jewish?"

"That's not the Kabala's Tree of Life," Des whispered. "It's a tree. Might be a pagan thing, like Yggdrasil."

"That would be consistent somewhere with more Germanic settlers than this region," Edmund muttered.

"Or it might be Native American," Des finished. "Climbing trees between the worlds is a shamanic thing. Know a bit about that myself."

"But that's not what worries me," Edmund whispered. "Some of those sigils are goetic."

"What do they have to do with goats?" I asked. Probably too loudly, but surprise has a tendency to make me loud.

"Not goats," Des said, much more quietly. "Goetic. As in of the *Goetia*. Part of the *Key of Solomon the King*."

"And we're back to Biblical," I said.

"We're back to *demons*," Edmund corrected me. "The spirits of the *Goetia* are often regarded as demons. And I see the sigil of at least Vassago, and, I believe Furfur."

"Where do they get these names?" I said.

"Not everyone regards them as demons," Des said.

"They're odd choices for a rootworker," Edmund countered.

"Only one way to find out," I said.

I turned and marched straight up to the door.

I raised my hand to knock.

The door opened before I could.

I was met first with a cackle.

And *this* was a cackle. High pitched, creaky with age, and full-throated. It went on and on as I tried to get a good look at the person making so much noise.

Looked to be the right age for a good cackle, but not nearly big enough a person to make so much sound.

She was short. Not more than five feet, and probably not that tall.

She was skinny. No. That's not enough. She looked like a skeleton someone had wrapped in skin, without first adding any meat. Maybe not even blood vessels. Because I couldn't see any on her arms, under her deep, nut-brown tan.

Her hair was white like snow, but it stuck out in all directions. Like someone had bleached wheat stalks brittle, then made a half-assed attempt at putting together a wig, before slapping it onto her head.

She wore a ... well, once upon a time it was a sundress. Blue, if I had to guess. It was gray now, and patched and stitched like Frankenstein's tailor had done a number on it.

Her eyes were so brown they were almost black. And they were boring into me even more than Edmund's had ever done.

"Well, well, well," she said, once her cackle was finished. From her tone of voice, though, it was never more than a hair more smile away from breaking through again. "If it isn't the vampire boy. What's the matter, boy? Got tired of living and wanted to pick the worst way to die that you could think of?"

"Why?" Edmund said, stepping up beside me. "Do you mean to kill him?"

"Don't need to," she said, looking Edmund up at down at least three times. "The vampire's on his trail. Won't be more than a few days. Maybe a week."

She drew her thumb across her throat and made a slashing sound.

She chuckled only a little though, and spat on her threshold, at my feet.

"We're here to keep that from happening," Edmund said. I think he was going to say more, too, but that was when the woman spotted Des.

She slammed the door.

Edmund and I looked at each other, both of us frowning.

"Heh," Des said. "Guess she's heard of my boys."

"Go away," she called through the door. "None of your starry wisdom around here. Get thee behind me!"

"Well," I muttered to Edmund, "that sounded Biblical to me."

"We're not Satanists," Des called through the door.

"I know what you are. You're worse."

"But—" I tried.

She cut me off.

"The Transmaniacon are not welcome here. And I've no help for any who work with them. Get off my land, or I'll send something to see you off."

"Please," I said.

"I don't—"

"Just listen!" I yelled.

"Then you'll go?" she asked.

"Then, if you wish me to leave, I will leave."

"Speak your peace."

She didn't open the door though. So I had to speak louder than I wanted to say things like I had to say.

"That vampire killed my friends."

"I know, you idiot. Who do you think saved your life?"

"I ... what?"

"Send your boy there away. I won't open that door until your Transmaniacon friend is back on his bike."

"Will inside our SUV do?" I asked.

That got her to open her door.

"You *left* your bike?" She said, words aimed straight at Des.

"This is that important," he said.

She cocked her head to one side. "No escape for you. You realize that. Without your bike—"

"I know what I'm in for."

The old woman nodded. "Back to your SUV then." She made a shooing motion. "Just 'cause you *might* be doing something noble doesn't mean I trust you a bit."

Des held up empty hands, and backed up all the way to the SUV. He jumped into the backseat. Closed the door. Held up his hands again.

The old woman nodded at me.

"I was there that night," she said. "Wasn't close enough to save your friends. Or powerful enough. Not with all that blood in the offing."

She looked down for a moment, as though she felt ashamed.

But there was no shame in her eye when she looked back at me.

"I was gathering some herbs that only grow near... Well, never you mind that. 'Taint your business."

"Fine," I said. "Why you were there is your concern."

"And I, of course, was smart enough to already have protection on me."

"What kind?" Edmund asked.

"Like I'd tell you." She snorted. "You want a charm, Mr. Moneybags, you can pay for it."

"How much would you like? For the three of us?"

"Wouldn't make a charm for a Transmaniacon. Not for all the gold in Fort Knox." She shook her head, then raised an eyebrow at me. "Too late for that one, I'm afraid. It's already got one hook into him. It'll get him through anything I can do."

She eyed Edmund again. Fluttered her eyelashes this time. "You and me, though, maybe we could work something out."

"If you cannot protect one friend of mine, and will not protect another, then you and I can do no business."

"Best you leave then," she said. "I've got chores."

"Wait," I said. "Please."

The please got her attention. She gave me a mollified look.

"This thing," I said. "It's coming to kill me. And if it does, it's going to keep doing what it's doing."

"That's what vampires are, boy."

"But if we kill *it*," I said, "the cycle stops. That's a lot of potential customers still alive to come to you for charms. You might not get any more money for mason jar protection spells, but I'm betting some customers will buy them anyway. Plus, I figure you have plenty of other business too."

"What makes you say so?" she said, eyes narrowed.

I smiled. Nice and wide.

"Dear lady," I said, "I worked in Hollywood for a long, long time. I've met more than my share of people who earn more per year than some countries' GNP. And one thing I've learned."

I gestured to Edmund. "Some people enjoy the luxuries of their money. It's the reason they have it, so they can enjoy it."

I pointed at her. "Others, they like to sock it away. Only use as much as they need to get by. To survive in the manner they're accustomed to."

I smiled again. "And I'm betting this" — I gestured to her house — "is how you grew up. I'm betting you don't need much."

I pointed up. "And your nice, new roof? Dead giveaway on a house like this one. So I'm also betting you've got enough socked away that you could buy all of Branson, if you wanted to. And that means business is good for you. With or without a vampire running around."

"What the hell would I do with a place like Branson?" Then she smiled at me. "Oh, but you're a clever one, though. Ain't you?"

I shook my head, just a little. "Can't be all that clever, going after a vampire. Doesn't mean I haven't learned a thing or two."

"All right, boy," she said through a rough chuckle. "I'll grant you. I've earned a dollar or two in my day, and I've got plenty of ways to make more."

She looked me up and down.

"All right," she said. "I'm not willing to do much here, because if you fail then the dead boy will come after me. I'll do you this much, though. Wait here."

She went back into her house, closing the door behind her.

I could hear her rummaging around, and complaining now and then as she did. More cats inside echoed her complaints.

But then she was back, and the door whipped open again.

"Now I'm not taking a dime from you, because I didn't do this. Understand? You tell anyone I gave you this, I'll send something to let you know you shouldn't have. Got me?"

I nodded.

"Right." She shoved something into my hand. "Now scat!"

She ducked back inside and slammed the door behind her. I could hear the locks click into place.

I looked down at what she gave me.

It was a sharpened dowel. Wood, sanded smooth. Flattened on the one end. Like, say, if it were ready to be hit by a mallet.

"That's holly," Edmund said. "Why would holly be the right wood for this? And where would she get holly around here? We're on the wrong side of the state for it to grow wild, and a proper stake must come from a wild tree."

"You think she doesn't know that?" I said with a smile.

"Point taken. Perhaps she gathered it for her own insurance."

"Doesn't matter why she had it." I twirled the dowel between my fingers. "I'd say we have our stake."

11

———————

As soon as we were back in the SUV, Des asked, "Was she any help? Or just a cryptic bitch?"

I held up the stake.

Des' face crinkled up with doubt.

"Holly." He said the word as though it tasted bad. "Doesn't seem likely, does it, Edmund?"

"No," Edmund said, holding out his hand. "I'd like to examine it as we drive, if you do not mind."

"Can you get us back all right?" Des asked.

"Yes, and yes," I said, handing over the stake and firing up the engine with a roar.

I admit it. I was starting to like having eight cylinders to play with. And the roads out this way were better than the ones I'd been driving out on the east side of Springfield. Though there were even more twists and turns.

Still, I kept us moving at a reasonable rate, as Edmund closed his eyes, holding the stake reverently before him.

"So," I said to Des, catching his eye in the rearview mirror. "We have things we need to talk about, you and I."

"Do we?" Des said, but I could hear in his voice he already knew what my first question was.

"Gonna make me ask?"

"No," he said, chuckling. "Let's get something straight right now. I'm not some kind of mind control artist. All right? I can't make you bark like a dog, or hand over all your hard earned cash, or any of that kind of thing."

"And yet," I said, leaning a little as I followed a sharp right curve, "I seem to recall my foot moving without my consent. Now how do you explain that?"

"Truth," Des said.

And he leaned back as though he considered that sufficient answer.

"Des?"

"Hmmm?"

"Do you agree that if we're going to fight a vampire together, we might just need to trust each other?"

"Are you saying I haven't earned your trust? Not even after what happened with the cops?"

"I'm saying I need more than answers like 'truth' or 'the knowledge beyond madness.'" I shook my head. "Otherwise, how can I be sure I won't hesitate at the wrong time?"

"Fine," he said with a sigh. "I hate explanations. Experience is so much better."

"And yet," I said, "I need to know what you meant by truth."

"Exactly what I said." He chuckled. "See, you wanted to follow that car. You knew as well as I did that whoever drove that Camry was following us, and with bad intentions. So ... I cut through the bullshit and prompted you to decide."

"That was all?"

"That's all I *can* do. In that way, anyway."

"So," I said, frowning as I tried to wrap my mind around this. "Say you're in a bar and you want to ask a girl to come home with you."

"Why do people always go straight to sex, when it comes to questions like this?"

He dug down around in the cooler, and came up with an Old Scratch IPA. A brand of beer that I knew for a *fact* hadn't been in there earlier.

He popped it open. Sipped. Caught my eye in the rearview and shook his head.

"Fine. That's your question." He shook his head again. Grimaced. Drank a little more beer. "It's flawed, because women usually *want* to take me home anyway, but all right. If I were asking a girl to come home with me, and I put the right amount of effort into it, I could cut through her internal back and forth until she reached the conclusion she wanted to reach anyway."

"So, if she was already inclined to want to sleep with you…"

"She'd be up for it. If she had *any* hesitation, she wouldn't." He shook his head again. "And anyone who needs any kind of power to get laid is a sad, sad case that probably could use a good ass-kicking."

"All right," I said. "Let's go a different direction then."

"Thank you."

"Suppose you'd used your power on that woman back there."

"That woman was a whole mess of contradictions. If I hit her with truth, I'm not sure what would come out the other side."

"What do you mean, 'hit her with truth?'"

"That's what I do. I don't control minds. I just cut through the bullshit to the truth. The truth back there was that you did want to follow that car. Your hesitation was a lifetime of societal training to assume the best in people. Or at least, to not assume the worst. Innocent until proven guilty. That kind of crap."

"Innocent until proven guilty is not crap!"

"It is outside of a courtroom."

Suddenly I was struck by the idea that Des was distracting me. Tricking my mind along different avenues than I wanted it to follow.

Because I wasn't done with my questions.

"Hey," I said.

"Good," he said, chuckling. "See, that's the other side of it. Distraction. People think the opposite of truth is falsehood, but it isn't. It's distraction. At least, in the larger sense."

"But lies—"

"Are just distractions from the truth. And largely, they're distractions we desire. That's what makes them both seductive, and dangerous." He sipped his beer, then added, "Which is why I keep talking about the knowledge beyond madness. It *is* truth, in the deepest sense. Because 'madness' is the world of distractions."

"Sounds Buddhist," I said. "Suffering, illusion and so on."

Des shrugged. "Not a Buddhist. Might be close, though our approach is ... condensed and intense. Still. Those guys go a long way to avoid distractions. More power to 'em."

"Speaking of distractions..."

He chuckled again, as I took us through a quick series of switchbacks that finally led to a paved road. Only a few more miles to actual freeway now.

"Why didn't you hit the cops with truth? If they were being controlled by a vampire, wouldn't it have freed them?"

"Tricky," Des said, tapping his jaw as he considered. "Problems with that approach. If they were allies of their own choosing, it might have gotten them from playtime to killing-us time with no room for us to maneuver."

He shook his head. "And if they *were* being controlled? That's a *lot* of distraction. Even if I'd been able to clear it with a single pass — and there's no guarantee I could — it might have snapped their minds."

I had to think about that one for a mile or two. Couldn't refute it, though. Even my doctors had warned against trying to unweave a delusion too quickly, and Des sounded a lot like he was talking about something similar. If more direct.

Made me think of something though.

"If you guys are all about the truth, then what exactly is the reputation of your little club? That woman seemed more worried about you than she was about the vampire."

"She can fight the vampire," Des said with a shrug. "Can't fight the truth."

"Ugh," I said, leaning forward against the heave of my stomach.

"Do you have *any* idea how lame that sounds?"

"Don't care," he said, and sipped more beer. "Truth is my thing. Not how it looks."

"Well, indulge me. Give me more here than truth."

"All right." Des chugged down the rest of his beer and let out a belch so loud it got Edmund to open his eyes for a moment.

Des chuckled, and Edmund went back to whatever he was doing. Then, finally, Des started to talk.

"Some people think we're angels. Others think we're devils. And still others think we're worse than either. If one of us shows up, that means the shit's hit the fan. If we show up in force, well..."

"Like Altamont?"

"Altamont." Des scoffed. "People blame us for Altamont. But they don't know what we averted that night."

"So, what, you're bogeymen?"

"Maybe." Des shrugged. "Point is, anyone who knows what we are, knows we've been through initiations they can't imagine. Or don't want to. They know we're into something deep."

Des grinned. "And they don't know for sure that we'll take their side, no matter which side is theirs."

"I thought you said, I mean, shit hitting the fan. That's bad, right? So you guys show up..."

"But what you think is bad isn't what Edmund thinks is bad. Or what that woman back there thinks is bad. Or those cops." Des shrugged. "See what I mean? Our perspective, it isn't like most people's."

"Give me an example," I said, not trying to hide that I thought he sounded like he was talking shit.

"Fine. The vampire. Right?"

"What's ambiguous about it? It needs to die."

"I'm with you there. But here's the thing." Des sat forward slightly. "Most people, they go after a vampire and they're going to try to save every life they can in the process. Me, I don't care about individual lives. I take a ... longer view. Every one of you will die and get reborn so many times that one more death, more or less, means less to me than this empty beer can."

Des crushed the can.

"But the vampire, that's different. The vampire, that's a thing that shouldn't be. Death is truth. Life is truth. And undeath is a distraction from truth." Des shook his head. "And worse than that, some manners of undeath, they break the death-rebirth cycle entirely."

A horn blared at me, and I had to jerk the wheel then to keep us on the road. It was paved now, and we were starting to see more afternoon traffic.

Fortunately, we were heading *into* Springfield during the start of the rush hour, and not out of it.

Don't get me wrong. What Missouri calls traffic makes Californians laugh. Their traffic is alike a slow drain, compared to a clog that backs up dirty water all over the bathroom floor.

Still. I needed to pay more attention to the road.

"I'm going to need to think about that one," I said.

"Too right you will," Des said, then chuckled. "Think things like this are understood in a moment? I'm telling you truths that philosophers have traded their souls for. And I'm not charging you a damn thing."

I kept us moving in a straight line now, as we began moving through what passed locally for a metropolis. Springfield. Stretched out, considering the population. But that just meant they had better parking and bigger lawns, though fewer restaurants that would interest me.

Well, there were other differences, but those were distractions.

And I had one more truth I had to ply from Des before we got back to the hotel.

"Go ahead," Des said, as though he'd read my mind.

If he could do that, though, I didn't want to know. I settled instead for the question I knew I wanted to ask.

"What the hell is 'starry wisdom?'" I gave him exactly long enough to open his mouth before saying, "And if you say, 'the wisdom of stars,' I'm going to floor it and swerve into oncoming traffic."

"Well, we can't have that, can we?" Des chuckled, and I flushed as I realized he'd just told me he didn't care about death. Or at least, not my death. And maybe not Edmund's.

"Just tell me," I said, exhaustion all through my voice.

"That's the thing," he said. "You don't really want to know."

This time it was my turn to get as far as opening my mouth before he continued.

"I'm not kidding." He shook his head. "Starry wisdom is the kind of thing you don't get to unlearn once you know it. And it changes the way you see the world forever. Maybe in ways you don't want."

"Des," I said, my tone flat, "if you think for a goddamn second this whole trip hasn't been one long adventure in learning things I don't get to unlearn, then you're not nearly as smart or as wise as you try to come across."

"Fuck brains, and fuck wisdom," Des said. "They're both distractions from the truth."

I could feel him stare at me from the backseat. But we were getting close to our exit now, and I didn't want to park without an answer.

"Fine," he said, and sighed. "I can't tell you. Exactly. But I can give you an idea. Think of it as one part astronomy, one part philosophy, and one part direct experience of the realities beyond the borders of our universe."

"Ooookay," I said. "Um, that doesn't really—"

"I'm not kidding," he said. "This universe is hardly the only one. It has a … kind of membrane that separates it from other planes of existence. The border of ours … it's a kind of … god, though I don't like the term and neither would it."

"So, the edges of our reality are sentient?"

"Sentient and sapient, in ways you couldn't begin to understand right now. There's a truth to it that might be beyond even my own understanding, and mine runs pretty deep. But there's always more to learn. To understand."

"So, what is this … not-quite-god?"

"Oh, some people have worshiped it as a god. Fools, mainly, since most of them don't understand the truly alien nature of it. All time, all space, all elements of this world, all are one in ... this being. And in passing through it, one gains the ability to travel the worlds, as it were."

I thought about that as I pulled into the valet parking section of the Usher hotel, right outside its glass doors.

I stopped the car. Looked back at Des.

"Passing through. That's the madness you have to cross. And starry wisdom is what you gain on the other side."

Des pointed his finger at me. Fired it like a gun.

"Bingo," he said.

12

———

WE HAD MAYBE THREE HOURS OF SUNLIGHT LEFT WHEN WE MADE IT
back to the suite. The whole place looked to have been cleaned and
polished in our absence.

"Wait," Des said, before I could get three steps inside the
main room.

Edmund practically stumbled at Des' command. I quickly
grabbed him by the shoulders and helped hold him steady.

"What?" I asked, my tone sharp. "Edmund needs rest, even more
than we do."

"I said wait," Des snapped, just as sharp.

Then he pushed Edmund and me back into the hall. Started to
close the door.

"Too late for that," Edmund said, and his voice sounded stretched.
Thin. Half-asleep already. "Anything that would have been triggered
by our entry has been triggered. But I detected nothing."

"*I* detect something," Des insisted. "But fine. Stay there while I
check things out."

I half-expected another graceful performance, like Edmund in
the graveyard.

I got nothing like that.

Des stomped around. Eyes wide open. Fists raised like he expected a fight every step of the way. I didn't see anyone else in the room, and from the impatience in Edmund's gray eyes, neither did he.

Still, Des stomped first to the couches and the windows. But if he found anything, I couldn't tell it.

Then over to the bar.

"Ha!" he said, and punched the air.

"Was that—" I tried to ask, but Edmund shook his head.

"When Des does something, you'll know it."

Des crouched behind the bar. Hefted up a case of bottles I didn't remember from before.

"Where did—"

But once more, I didn't get the question out.

"Ordered 'em myself," Des said. "Always prefer Teufelsbrau, when I can get it. But somebody tried to tag my order."

Des clapped his hands above the case of beer bottles.

When his hands came together, thunder roared. A blast of hot air staggered me back a step. Almost knocked Edmund out of my hands, but the man seemed to weigh half of nothing.

"That's one," Des said, holding up one middle finger, pointed toward the windows."

"Maybe that's all?" I ventured, but weakly. I sure wasn't going to interrupt him now.

Des stomped over to our bedroom doors. And maybe it was just my imagination. Or maybe it was the aftermath of that thunderclap. But each stomping step of Des' seemed to echo now. As though he wore steel shoes instead of motorcycle boots, and stomped not on carpet, but on marble.

At each door, another "Ha!" another punch, and another thunderclap.

Des went inside each room, and I didn't stop him. More thunderclaps.

He came back out dusting his hands.

"I'd say it's safe now." He gestured for us to enter.

I helped Edmund into his room. Helped him sit on his bed.

"I'll hold this," he said, holding up the holly stake. "If you don't mind. There are tests I can do while dreaming."

That made just about no sense to me at all. I knew a thing or two about lucid dreaming. Todd used to go on about it at length, and even Tangi used to claim he could do it.

But they both agreed that lucid dreaming was a chancy thing. Hard to guarantee a lucid dream on any given night, even for an experienced lucid dreamer. The talent or skill was supposed to be subject more than a little to the whims of the subconscious. Apparently even skilled lucid dreamers might go months at a time without achieving lucidity in a single dream.

But after all I'd seen lately, there was no way in hell I was going to try to correct Edmund.

If he said he could do it, I was ready to believe he could.

I let him keep the stake, and rejoined Des in the main room of the suite.

He was sitting on the couch, an open beer bottle in his hand, his boots up on the coffee table, and a broad, shit-eating grin on his face.

"Let me guess," he said. "More questions?"

"Just one," I said. "What were you getting rid of?"

"Distractions, mostly," he said. "Triggers of alarms, though I might have set them off in the process. I don't think I did, but it's hard to be too sure. Nature of the beast, you know. Alarms carry truth, even when the methods of placement are all about distraction."

I stared at him, trying to parse some useful information out of his words.

He grinned back at me. Sipped his beer.

"Talking to you, Des, is like tuning the radio while driving cross-country. And just about as likely to give me anything I want to hear."

Des started laughing. I think he was going to say something else, but I waved my hand to stop him.

All that really mattered was that some kind of traps had been laid for us, and Des got rid of them. Of course, by his own admission he might have alerted our enemies in the process. But apparently that was the cost of doing business.

All I could hope was that, when they got there, we'd all be rested and ready.

So I slammed the door to my room, threw myself on my bed, and did some strategic napping.

I BOLTED AWAKE OUT OF DARK, HEAVY SLEEP. MY BODY REFUSED to move.

I couldn't even shake my head. Twitch my feet. Raise my hands. Nothing.

I was frozen in place. Laying face-down across my bed. Covers all still up.

Well, not quite face-down. My face was pointed to one side. But my belly was on the bedspread.

Someone was pounding on my door. But how had anyone gotten into my apartment? Why would they be pounding on my bedroom door?

For that matter, why was my bedroom door closed? I never closed it.

And why couldn't I move?

More pounding knocking.

"Sel!" Des' voice. "Get your ass out here. Time to wake up. We have business."

Wait.

Des.

This wasn't my bedroom. This wasn't my apartment.

I was in my room in our suite. Usher Hotel. Springfield, Missouri.

That explained the absolute darkness of the bedroom. They had blackout curtains here. I didn't have any at home.

That also explained the vaguely floral scent to the air. The cool air conditioning, which I definitely didn't have at home.

Didn't explain why I couldn't move.

That made sweat break out on my forehead. Why couldn't I move?

I tried. Tried to shimmy. Just move my whole body at once. Couldn't do more than blink. Move my eyes.

Worse, I could feel pressure on my back now...

No. That wasn't a spirit. Incubus, succubus, hag or anything else. Those things weren't real.

Sleep paralysis. That was real.

The pounding knock came again. Reassuring in its way. Had to have jolted me awake. Maybe even out of a dream. My body was still paralyzed, expecting to keep me from acting out my dreams.

There was nothing on my back.

That pressure was an illusion. Hallucination. Distraction. A lie.

And that faint noise I heard, under the pounding knock. That was just the air conditioning.

I didn't hear breathing.

A terrifying *crack* of wood breaking.

The door to my room burst open.

Des, charging like he was coming in to tackle me. Even though I was already down.

Des, diving through the air above my prostrate form.

Des, wrestling with something on the bed beside me.

I could move now. My limbs felt like lead, but I could move.

And I could see what Des wrestled with.

It was small. Maybe half the height of a human, but it had the right kind of limbs and fingers. Its naked skin was green, mottled and translucent. Its body was hideous. Bloated. Neckless. And the head had a huge, gaping mouth, and nothing like hair, or even a normal skull line.

I tried to help. Tried to punch. Moved so slowly I tagged Des in the kidney instead. Might have mattered, if there'd been anything behind the punch.

I fell back on the bed, panting.

Des managed to get the thing underneath him. Began squeezing where its neck should have been, while mumbling something in a language I wasn't sure I ever wanted to understand.

Finally, the thing popped. Like a soap bubble, but three or four times as slimy.

Hot, greenish goo all over my skin.

I'm not proud of what I did then.

I scrambled backwards, trying for speed and failing. Flailing at the goo with dull hands that couldn't manage anything like agility or dexterity.

I fell hard to the floor. Cricked my neck and banged my head. All the while worried that this goo was seeping through my pores. Infecting me. Making me like that thing.

Then my worst fears were confirmed.

Des. Standing over me. Covered in goo. Clearly turning into whatever that thing was.

Reaching for me.

But I wasn't going down without a fight.

I threw up a punch with everything I could put behind it. The most coherent idea I'd had since awakening.

And apparently that made a difference.

I cracked Des across the jaw.

"Ow!" he said, pulling back his hand. "Jeez. Try to help a guy."

"But you're ... aren't you ... what's happening?"

"Oh." Des chuckled. "That, my friend, was an *actual* hag. And it was trying to leech out your life. Either all of it, or enough to make your blood easy prey for the vampire. I figure the latter, though that couldn't have made you a good meal. But there are things about different breeds of vamp that I don't know, and I'm betting this is one of them. Never thought a vamp would work with a hag, anyway. They seem too similar in..."

And that point he must have seen me trying to throw the time-out gesture.

"Gonna hit me if I offer you a hand?"

"Are you turning into a hag?"

That got a knee-slapping laugh out of Des.

"No more than you, my friend. And you aren't. I assure you. Hags don't reproduce that way."

Part of me wanted to ask how they did. More of me didn't want to know.

I nodded.

Des helped me up.

"How you doing?" He looked me up and down. "I'm thinkin' it can't be good."

"I feel…" I shook my head. Tried to get rid of the last of my sleep. "I feel like I've been run over by a fleet of trucks."

"Damn," he said. "Means it got to you sooner than I sensed it. Sorry."

I started wiping at the goo.

"Don't bother," he said. "It'll dissolve soon enough. Won't even leave residue."

"Page and Todd'll be pissed," I muttered.

That got Des to look sharper at me.

"I know they're dead," I said. "I just…"

"I get it," he said, and laid a gentle hand on my shoulder.

I took a quick assessment. I'd hit my head, but not too hard. Had a hell of a kink in my neck. Most of my body felt like it had been wrung out and hung on a clothesline, then yanked down and driven over by a fleet of … not just trucks. Tanks.

Glancing over at my doorway told me Des had kicked the door open. Broke the door frame in the process.

But I didn't remember locking it…

I almost asked about that, but didn't bother. If hags were real, and obviously they were, then it must have locked the door.

"What were you saying about having business?"

"Oh, that," Des said, shaking his head. "Anger scares away a lot of nasties, if you do it right, and I wasn't sure what was in here with you."

"Time is it?" I asked.

"Close to sundown and almost dinner time. Was just about to wake Edmund, when—"

"I'm here," Edmund said from the doorway. He strode straight to me.

Without another word, Edmund grabbed my hands. Inspected my palms. Then the backs of my hands.

He stepped behind me. Moved his hands over the back of my neck. Checked out more of me from behind. Felt clinical in the weirdest way.

"Raise your right foot," Edmund said, walking back around to my front.

I did.

"Set it down. Now right hand high and left hand straight out."

"Should I do the hokey-pokey and turn myself around?"

"Please," Edmund said. "Just humor me."

I did.

"Not too much then," Edmund said to Des. "And I can replenish what he has lost." Edmund turned to me then. "I cannot undo the kink in your neck though. I'd recommend a massage, normally, but under the circumstances…"

"Under the circumstances," Des said, "none of the three of us should be alone again until this is over. Maybe not even in the bathroom."

"And I'll wish to cleanse this room, and renew some of my protections."

"When did…" I started, but I let the question go. There was no point. Of course Edmund had laid protections. Probably Des tool.

Just like hags were real, and one had tried to eat me.

"We'll need to fortify tonight," Des said. "I'm not even sure we should leave."

"No," I said. "They just proved they can get to us right here."

"But if we fortify—"

"If we fortify, they'll get us kicked out. Or they'll … corrupt the cleaning staff." I shook my head. "If we think we're strong, they'll hit us where we're weak."

"You do raise a good point," Edmund said, gently, "but it means you must go out after dark."

"I know," I said, and my body was too exhausted for my heart to begin pounding its objection the way it normally would to such an idea.

I grimaced. "It's time."

13

———————

Emotionally, I wanted to run out the door, Des and Edmund trotting right behind me. Maybe while dramatic music swelled, and we went to a series of cut scenes of the three of us, hitting the streets. Looking for trouble, and handling anything we could find. Beating up the right kinds of lowlifes to get the right clues, so we could go straight to taking down the Big Bad and saving the day.

But life just never worked out the way I wanted it to.

Or maybe I spent too many years working in film and television.

Then again, maybe it was just that I'd had something like half of my life force sucked out by a hag.

So I got as far as turning toward the door of my room — not even our suite, which somehow made this fact sting all the more — and got maybe one step before I broke out in a cold sweat, and had to have my trembling, panting body caught by Des before it hit the floor.

Des laid me out on my bed like I weighed less than Edmund. I tried to think that was just because the gray-haired old biker was that strong, and not because the hag had somehow been devouring actual chunks of my body.

Edmund then sent Des out of the room. I think it was to order dinner for us, but he might have already done that. A little extra fortification before we went out.

Maybe it was just to clear the psychic field of the room. I could imagine Des as being the kind of guy who carried a big aura around with him.

Either way, lying there on the bed felt wonderful. I wanted to sleep, but couldn't. And not because of the stabbing pain in my neck, either. My eyes just refused to stay closed.

"You're rested," Edmund said gently. He removed his suit jacket and hung it up, continuing to talk on his way back to my bedside. "What you need is not rest. What you need is life force."

"Wha..." I couldn't even get the whole word out before my jaw started shaking. In fact, all of me started shaking, like I was cold. Even though I'd only set the air conditioning to a moderate seventy-four.

"Shh," Edmund said. "The hag was devouring you from the aura in. It punched a hole, if you will."

Edmund began to wave his hands slowly over my body. Maybe three feet above my physical body.

"Here," he said, stopping just over my chest. "Here is the hole it made. A ring, torn all the way around, to facilitate the way it feeds."

"B..." I couldn't even get out the word "but," and yet Edmund seemed to either read my mind or knew what question I'd ask.

"Shh," he said again. "What matters is not how it got in, nor how it feeds. What matters is how we fix what has been done to you."

He waved his right hand through a series of quick, sure gestures.

"I'm not sure if you've heard of Reiki," he said.

I managed a shaky nod. I was sweating even worse now. Not because I was worried about Reiki. Just because, well, just because I was still leaking life force out of the hole ripped in my aura by a hag.

Wow. I thought just getting those words out would help. Nope. Still felt crazy.

Reiki, though, was a Japanese practice. A...

"A way of tuning into the universal flow of Ki," Edmund said, as though I'd shaken my head instead of nodding. But his hands were steady above me now. And as he continued talking, I began to feel a ... flow of warmth from his hands into my chest.

"Each of us possesses our own Ki," Edmund continued, "but places also have Ki. And the universe itself has Ki, that flows along channels and meridians. Through us. With us. There are entire systems taught about the flow of Ki, and how one may flow with it."

"Q-Q-Q-Qi g-g-g-g—"

"Qi Gung, yes," he said, and the flow was growing hot. Nevertheless, I stopped sweating. And the heat was spreading as warmth throughout my body.

"I am not a practitioner of those more refined systems. Qi Gung. Tai Chi. Acupuncture, and the like. However, I have found a derivation of Reiki that proves quite useful in my particular way of working. It has the added benefit of replenishing others without draining anything from me. As I believe you are beginning to feel?"

I nodded, and felt more sure of myself as I did.

And that realization made my eyes open wide.

"Yes," Edmund said, smiling, as he adjusted the position of his hands in the air above me. "When the hag dined on the flow of your life energy, your Ki, it dined also on your sense of self."

He met my eyes for a moment. "I found it most impressive that you were capable of action. Of making the decision to face your fears and go out into the night. Even though you were lacking much of yourself at the time."

He nodded, then went back to looking at ... whatever the hell he was looking at as he continued *repairing my Ki*.

Nope. Still felt weird to say.

"However," Edmund continued, "as the universal flow of Ki refreshes your life force, you will find that your sense of self and your certainty returns. Perhaps even stronger than ever, in much the way that a bone, once broken, knits stronger at the break point."

That didn't sound likely to me. I didn't see how getting dined on by a hag could make my "aura" stronger.

Then again, even though I was feeling more like myself, I was having to admit that there was indeed, more in heaven and earth than dreamt of in my philosophy...

And before I knew it, Edmund was finished.

I felt as though I'd actually had a good, solid nap. Or maybe several hours of refreshing sleep.

I was still hungry, and my neck still ached (though less than before, unless I was mistaken), but I was ready to go see about a vampire.

"Ah," Edmund said as I jumped to my feet. "I'd say you're feeling better then."

"Good," Des said from the doorway. "The food just got here."

ROOM SERVICE BROUGHT US A PRETTY GREAT DINNER. WHATEVER ELSE the Usher did, it did food right.

All three of us had mixed vegetables that were spiced in ways that just made them pop in my mouth.

And for the main course, Des and I had steaks. Rib eyes. Rare and bloody, which, by all rights, should have turned me off. What with us going after a creature that wanted to feast on my blood.

But I was so hungry that all I could think about was how good that steak tasted. Done the way it was, with just the right amount of pepper, and some combination of other subtle spices that made it disappear off my plate faster than I would have believed.

Edmund's river trout vanished in a slower, more elegant fashion. But I wasn't worried about that. Maybe I had more reason to be hungry than he did.

They also gave us some pretty fantastic garlic bread.

I was just sopping up the rest of my meat juices with some garlic bread when Des — only half-done with his own steak — chuckled and said, "Do you want to tell him, or should I?"

Edmund inclined his head.

"After effect of that kind of experience," Des said. "Food tastes better because of the fresh flow of life energy." He popped a bite of steak into his own mouth and added, while chewing, "Also, the loss and replenishment makes demands on the body that can only be handled with food."

"Whatever," I said. I wasn't sure how much I really wanted to know about all this. And we had something more important to talk about. "What's the plan?"

Des grimaced at Edmund, who gave him a cold look.

"What?" I asked.

"We have had something of a disagreement about the proper approach to this particular situation," Edmund said. He sipped a little white wine. "And perhaps you could help him see reason."

"Or maybe," Des said, gulping down a little beer to clear his own mouth, "you can make this guy realize there's only one proper way to handle this."

I sipped a little of my own soda. Sighed.

"All right," I said. "Tell me, one at a time. No interruptions. Make your cases. I'll decide."

"I'm not sure—" Des started, but Edmund spoke over him.

"Sel is the one most in danger. The one the creature most seeks. I agree that he should make the decision about our approach, and I will stand by his decision, even if I disagree."

Des rolled his eyes. "Fine. Sel makes the call."

"Thank you," Edmund said. He sipped a little more white wine, then made his case.

"Tonight is when you are in the most possible danger." Edmund set down his silverware — actual *silver*ware. "The fiend will be at its strongest. It will have the most potential allies to call upon. It will seek you out in the time and place most to its advantage. Thus, it is incumbent on us to deny it these advantages."

Edmund held up one finger. "First, we must find the safest place for you throughout this night. I believe that would be the closest Catholic church, for you were baptized and raised in that faith, even if your faith has lapsed."

He raised a second finger. "Second, we must take such measures as Des and I can take to fortify that location. To deny the fiend its allies, even as your location should deny it direct access."

He raised a third finger. "Third, I spend the night remote viewing the fiend. Taking such measures as I can to find it, and track it back to its lair. This will tell us not only where to find it when it is weak, but should provide us with a sense of its own safeguards, that we might foil them."

Edmund nodded at Des to signify that he was finished.

"May I rebut?" Des asked, in formal tones that really did not suit his Hells Angel look.

"If I may rebut your case," Edmund said.

"Fine," Des said. Then dropped the mock formality. "Every hunter since the dawn of time has played it that way. And every vampire since the dawn of time knows that's how hunters like to work. If we go that route, it will have planned for us in ways we can't foresee. Plus, it blocked Edmund's remote viewing before, which means it knows we have that capability. It may lay a false trail, and we wouldn't know until the trap is sprung."

"Counterpoint," Edmund said, eyebrows raised at me.

"One," I said. "Or we'll be sitting here until it comes for me."

"I believe I may have discovered a way to penetrate its defenses."

"And," Des said, "if I wanted to lay a trap for you, that's just what I'd let you think."

Edmund drew breath to say something, but I still both he and Des with raised hands.

"What's your approach, Des?"

"We pick a nice open area. A secluded park, by preference. We set up what defenses we can, and we wait. It'll come to us. And yes, it'll be at its strongest, but to play off your point — if it thinks its strong, we'll show it where it's weak."

Edmund opened his mouth to speak.

"Not done yet," Des said.

Edmund nodded.

"It won't know we have the holly. We can be sure that the old witch had some ways of keeping information from it, or it would have gone after her by now. So we have a means to kill it that it doesn't know we have."

Des grinned. "Now, I'm betting that if we clearly set ourselves up as a challenge, it'll come right at us itself. Not waste time with allies. After all, it's likely confident in its power. But we have an edge it doesn't expect. And that's why we'll win."

"Finished?" Edmund asked.

Des nodded.

"Meanwhile," Edmund said, "the vampire, which we know is nearly swift as thought, will likely kill Sel before Des can drive home the stake."

"We know the vamp likes to savor its kills," Des said. "You guys had plenty of time to plug away with bullets while it killed Todd Jeffries. I might have time to stake it before it finishes Sel."

"Might," Edmund said. "Not a chance I'm willing to live with."

"If you're both finished," I said.

They turned and looked at me. Both of them ready to hear my verdict. Ready to know which plan I favored. Which way we'd go after the vampire.

I raised a finger.

"You both agree," I said, "that I make the final call about how we do this?"

Both men nodded.

"Good," I said. "Because both those approaches suck. I have a much better idea in mind."

By the time I was done telling them, Des was laughing, and Edmund was frowning in thought.

But they both agreed to go along with it.

After all, it was *my* neck first on the chopping block.

14

————————

Des drove the SUV. After all, he was the one who knew where we were going. Edmund in the front seat. Me in the backseat.

Each of them were carrying a few things they thought they'd need. Me, all I had worth talking about was the stake.

Des had wanted to hold onto the stake, but that whole "my neck on the chopping block" argument helped. Of course the "it killed my friends" argument was the one that got him to hand over the stake.

And the stake was the right weapon. Edmund was sure of that now. He'd done some kind of dream work to puzzle it through, and he had given me a longwinded explanation, but to be honest, the explanation needed an explanation, far as I was concerned.

All I really got out of Edmund's longwinded talk were three things.

One, the stake could kill this vampire, if driven through its heart.

Two, the stake would vanish with the vampire.

Three, Edmund had increased my chances of hitting the heart on my first shot.

I didn't follow that part of the explanation at all. It involved probabilities, on one level, but also my own innate athleticism as far as I was concerned.

As far as Edmund was concerned, there was a whole slew of other factors that had to be enhanced or eliminated. And he'd done a lot of enhancing and eliminating.

All I really cared about was the first thing. I could kill the vampire with this holly stake.

We were all three dressed for war.

Me, I was freshly showered and wearing a blue *Seekers* tee shirt, with the logo in white. I wore tan cargo shorts, and my best running shoes. I had free and easy movement, and the shirt was my tie to my friends.

I'd need them with me tonight. Even took a moment to pray before I put on that shirt. Pray that my friends were in heaven. Pray that they were watching over me. That maybe, just maybe, I could get a little divine help in ending this unnatural thing.

Des was in his leathers. All weathered and old, like him, but all still strong and ready for action. Also like him. Under his club vest, he wore a gray Harley Davidson tee shirt.

I don't know. Maybe it was a holy relic.

Edmund dressed in a simple gray suit, with a narrow, black tie over a crisp white shirt. He looked polished. High class. Like he should never have been found within a hundred miles of the place we were going.

I also knew that he had things in his pockets. Little preparations of his own.

Des didn't look like he was carrying anything. But I was sure, if I asked, he'd have told me that trinkets were distractions from the truth. Or something like that.

We were still driving when the sun went down.

Made it easier, at first. I was still behind a window, watching the darkness rise on the streets around me. Between cars in the traffic. The extra luster it added to the stoplights. The flicker and glow of the streetlights.

Shadows, shadows everywhere, and not a spot to think.

All I could do in the moment was watch those shadows. Watch

the way they spread between cars. Between pedestrians, crossing at a red light. The way even the sky itself seemed a great shadow.

Which it was. The light of our sun blocked by the rotation of our own planet.

I was literally looking at the earth's shadow in the night sky.

I tried to distract myself with thoughts like that. Even fully aware that Des would remind me that I was enjoying the distractions from the truth. And it was the truth I needed to deal with.

But I would face that truth soon enough.

Right now, I needed to not think about the tension filling my stomach. The tightness in my balls. The jittery feeling in my legs, making my knees hop-hop-hop as we drove. The way I pulled against the seatbelt to feel the pressure. The way my fingers danced and fidgeted on the armrest and on the seat beside me.

The first beads of sweat on my forehead.

I wanted to call it off. Take Edmund's route. Find a church and hide in it like a goddamn child scared of the dark.

Even though I wasn't scared of the dark.

I was scared of the things out there *in* the dark.

Things that I knew now were all too real.

But damn it, my time for hiding was done. My time for watching from safety was done.

One way or the other, the end would come tonight.

One way or the other, I would no longer fear the dark. Not after tonight.

By the dawn, either I would be dead, or the vampire.

I would not accept a third option.

DES ROLLED US TO A STOP ALONG A STREET THAT LOOKED WAY TOO deserted to be the right place. There were no more than two other cars parked on the whole block, and one of them looked abandoned.

"Des?" I asked, but before I could get out the rest of the question, he answered.

"This is the right place." He turned and grinned at me over the seat. "Most people stay away from here after dark. Survival instinct, even if they don't know it. And the things that come here, most of them don't drive cars."

"The ghoul did."

"Fine," Des said with a frown. "Most of them don't *usually* drive cars."

He shook his head and got out of the car. Edmund joined him at the same time.

They closed their doors, Des with a slam and Edmund with a simple click.

And me, I was still in the backseat.

"Come one, Sel," I muttered. "It's just the nighttime. It's just your life."

The sun was gone now. The sky above was still darkening with twilight. Not yet full night. But still, the sun was gone.

I knew what that meant.

Des knocked on my window, making me jump. Edmund stilled him with a hand on the shoulder.

I looked straight up, past the roof of the SUV. Addressed my dead friends. "Guys, if you can hear me, this is for you."

I opened the door and got out.

The night air was still warm from the hot day. And still muggy. Didn't smell like growing things though. Not here. Here is smelled like neglect: oil and urine, old garbage. Those kinds of smells. None of them strong enough to be all that close, but none of their sources all that distant either.

The night ... should have been different. Should have felt as pregnant with weirdness as what we were about to do. But it didn't.

It all just felt so goddamn ordinary that the hairs on the back of my neck stood up. Made me roll my shoulders.

My stomach still puckered a bit, objecting to what I was doing. And my balls, they were still thinking of crawling back up inside my body.

But I steadied myself through a breath, and looked back and forth along the closed and abandoned storefronts, looking for our destination.

I was glad the place looked abandoned. Glad there weren't likely to be innocent people caught up in what was going to go down.

Still. This block, it looked as though it couldn't have the kind of place we needed.

There were six stores on the block. At the far corner, a great big pharmacy, long since closed. Two of the windows were broken, and no one had bothered to board them up.

A dry cleaner was next, and it looked as though it might still have been in business. The hair dresser next to it — the Hair-Care Affair — gave up a while ago. All their windows were boarded up. Three had bullet holes.

Three little restaurants next. All closed.

Down at the end of the block, a liquor store. At least, that's what we'd call it in California. Wasn't sure if there was some local name for them here in Missouri, the way there was in Michigan, where they called them "party stores."

That place was still open. Lights in the windows, neon beer signs, and everything. No cars, but they had their own lot...

"The liquor store?" I asked.

"Nope," Des said. "Want to guess again?"

"Must we?" Edmund said. "I'd prefer not to waste time with games while we're being observed."

I would have spun around, looking for the observer, but Des stopped me with a "casual" hand on the shoulder before I could.

"Best time for games," Des said through a smile. "Shows aplomb."

"What—" I started.

"Where we are right now," Des said, still smiling, "is the kind of place that gets watched. Any humans in the area, they're predators of their own kind. And the things that aren't human, they're bigger predators yet. Key here is not looking like prey."

"Sel," Edmund said to Des, "smells more than enough like prey. There's no need to pretend to behaviors that do not suit us."

"Either way," I said, rolling my shoulders and trying to get my heart rate under control. No. Check that. I was trying to persuade myself that my heart rate was elevated due to excitement. Even anger.

But definitely not fear.

"Either way," I tried again, and this time I could finish the sentence, "we might as well stroll in. Any watchers probably know who I am, and that I'm here. Word will reach our enemy soon enough. If it hasn't already."

Des and Edmund both nodded. No surprise. After all, the reason all of Edmund's allies had turned away from him was supposed to be that everyone knew I was in town and that the vampire was coming for me.

That meant that everyone who could see such things, could identify me.

Hell, I was counting on that for my plan to work.

"So where are we going?" I asked.

"Sure you don't want one more guess?" Des asked with a broader grin.

"Oh, for the sake of every saint's blood," Edmund said, then stepped quickly to the closed hairdresser's.

He gestured at one of the wood panels overlaying the old windows.

"No fun at all, *Eddie*," Des said, leading me over, one hand still on my shoulder.

With his free hand, Des knocked on the wood panel Edmund had indicated. The leather of his gloves should have muted the sound, but I would have sworn it managed a faint echo on the street.

Or maybe that was because the street was so quiet. The buzz of traffic was distant. Background. And under that, only hints of night-time insects about their rounds.

The board slid an inch to one side.

"Password," a rough voice said.

"Fours winds, but the windows are barred."

Edmund's head nearly snapped off his body, fast as he looked at Des.

Des gave a small shake of his head against whatever question Edmund wanted to ask.

"Works for you," said the rough voice. "But not for them."

"Since when?"

"Maybe since tonight."

"Let us in," Des said, leaning forward and voice full of menace, "or I'll start to huff and puff, and we'll see what it takes to blow your house down."

"Careful, Transmaniacon," the rough voice said. "Might not want that much trouble."

"When have any of my boys steered away from trouble?"

Silence for a moment. I thought I could hear voices somewhere ahead of us.

"Has to be this way?"

Des nodded.

"Let me check."

The panel slid back into place.

Des kicked it open.

"Hey!" the rough voice said.

I could see the speaker now. Saying he'd seen better days didn't begin to cover it. And just the sight of him turned my stomach. Made me worry I'd lose that wonderful steak all over the entryway.

I was looking at a dead man. He was standing. Expressive even, in his displeasure. But decidedly, unquestionably *dead*.

First of all, he was rotting.

Most of his lanky black hair was missing. Half the flesh of his face was gone down to yellowed bones, and the other half was bulbous and looked as though it might start to slide down onto his neck at any moment.

His neck didn't even have that much flesh on it. Looked as though most of it had rotted away, starting at a horizontal line across the middle, and spreading outwards, both up and down.

No wonder his voice was so rough.

The fists he held up were grayed flesh, with bone showing through in places.

And what he wore must have been the clothes he was buried in. Seersucker suit, almost as decrepit as he was.

I should have been able to smell all that rot. I couldn't though, which might have been the only reason my gorge never got as high as my throat.

Des stepped through. I braced myself and followed, Edmund right behind me.

"I gave the password," Des said. "The right password for anyone of my club. It's always been good enough for me and guests before. So don't bullshit me about checking with management."

"Not the same situation," the dead man said, his white, milk-of-magnesia eyes flicked to me and back. "Needs approval. Wait the fuck outside."

"Let us in," Des said, "or I'll hit you with enough truth to disintegrate what's left of your carcass."

"Do it," the dead man said with a shrug. "Free me from this bondage and let me die."

Des leaned forward, and I could hear the evil grin in his voice.

"Oh, no," Des said. "you'll still be bound. The bond is a form of truth. You'll just be dust. Useless to your master, but why would he bother releasing you? You won't exactly be in the way…"

"Fine," the dead bouncer said, hands coming up in surrender. "Fine. You three can come in. Can't say you'll be popular inside though."

"Leave that to our sparkling personalities," Des said.

And the three of us continued down the hall.

THAT THIS WAS A HALL DIDN'T MAKE SENSE TO ME. AFTER ALL, everything I'd seen from the front made it clear that this was an ex-hairdresser's. Should have been a big room in the front with tile floor, or linoleum maybe, and plenty of space for chairs and stations and all that kind of thing.

But I'd long since given up expecting my life to make sense.

Instead, there was a white speckled linoleum floor all right. But the walls on either side, those were white, speckled linoleum too. As though someone had folded the floor up on both sides to make the hallway.

But the ceiling, it was distant. Too far away to see in the dim, sourceless light.

I didn't like the dim, sourceless light, either. I wanted to know where the little bit of light we got was coming from. Wasn't behind us. The panel slid closed, and there was no sign of the street back there. Just solid wall.

I wasn't even sure how that panel had slid closed. Des had kicked it open.

Was any of this real? Any of it at all?

There was a dead man, rotting away, but he could stand and talk and offer insults and hold up his fists like he wanted to fight.

I was walking through a closed building that was cool. Not hot and muggy like the evening. No. Cool and dry. Without the whir of an air conditioner. Without any reason I could determine for the change.

I was walking through a hall that shouldn't have been there. And the floor, folded up like walls, but squared off like it was always built that way.

I kept whipping my head around. Looking for anything that made sense. Wondering if my heart rate was going to slow down, or if I was going to end up going into cardiac arrest.

Maybe I was still inside. Back in that hospital.

Maybe I'd never gotten released at all. Maybe my delusions had just grown too strong. Overwhelmed reality. Made me dream of years of something like a normal life, but my mania was too strong. Brought it all crashing back down.

Maybe I was seeing everything Page and Todd told me about because I was so guilty over their deaths.

I couldn't get enough air.

Why couldn't I get enough air?

I stopped walking. Crouched. Lowered my head, far as I could. Put my hands on the cold, dusty linoleum.

How could it be dusty? A dead man walked across it, even before Des did.

I started laughing. Without any air, I started laughing. A gasping, wheezing sound. My heart pounding so hard I could feel it in my throat. In my thighs. In my wrists and ankles.

This was it. I was going to die right here. The delusions had overcome me at last. My guilt had done its job, after years — or maybe just weeks.

Maybe there never was an asylum.

Maybe I've been in a coma all this time. Blood loss and brain damage from the concussion.

Maybe I was about to die from my wounds that night.

Maybe—

"Selwyn Robertson," Des said, and his voice reverberated all the way down to my very soul. "Look around yourself and see *truth*."

My eyes blinked so fast the dull light strobed.

I wasn't in the hospital. I wasn't in the asylum either.

I was in that odd hallway inside what was once a hairdresser's. I could smell old hair tonic and hair. Only the vaguest hints, but they were there.

Just that little fact alone made my heart lurch and slow to a more normal rate. Stilled the sweat I hadn't realized had begun pouring off of me. Sticking my shirt to my torso and my hair to my head.

I understood the light now. The light came from dim bulbs, off at the top of the high ceiling. I couldn't quite see them, but I could tell now by the dull glow they shed, where they were and where they weren't.

The linoleum floor truly was folded into the hallway we were walking down.

And the dead man ahead of me, he was a zombie of some variety. A corpse brought back to life to serve his master. I could almost see the puppet strings leading off of his limbs. Faint sparks of thread, going down the hall ahead of him.

I could see Edmund now. See the worry in those gray eyes, but see the worry settling down as I looked back at him.

Edmund, he was limned in a greenish-purplish light. That light was his aura. I wasn't sure how I knew that, but it was true. And that combination of colors told me that Edmund was exactly as he presented himself to me. He was a psychic. And he was a man who tried to leave the world a better place than he found it, everywhere he went.

I turned to look at Des, who had managed to keep himself just outside my peripheral vision as I turned around and around to see the truth.

"Stop," Des said, his tone just as commanding.

And just like that, I couldn't see where the light bulbs were anymore. And I couldn't see Edmund's aura, and the dead man just looked like a dead man.

I could see Des though. He stepped in front of me, staring deep into my eyes, checking on me.

"But—" I started, but Des stopped me by shaking his head.

"Trust me," he said. "You aren't ready to see the truth of me. And you won't want to see the truth of the things you're likely to see in this bar."

I nodded. I trusted him now. Completely. Not because I had to. I could tell there was no compulsion on me. Or at least, I was as sure as I could be that there wasn't.

No, it was the simple matter that he'd shown me truth. And anyone who had the power to do that, well, he didn't seem like the sort who was going to lie to lead me into a trap.

This was a scary thing I was doing. But I was going into it with the right two people at my back.

And even more important than that fact? That I now knew, with bone-deep certainty, that all this was really happening.

Somewhere, deep down, I'd been doubting that. Without even knowing I was doubting it. But now I knew without the slightest doubts that it was real. That my friends had died just the way I remembered.

And that meant I really could avenge their deaths.

"Look," the dead man said, "are you guys coming in or not?"

"We're coming," I said, my voice certain.

THE BAR ITSELF WAS A DISAPPOINTMENT.

I wasn't sure what I was looking forward to seeing. Maybe a scene out of *The Monster Club*, where werewolves were drinking from smoking glasses and howling at ghouls who gnawed on leg bones and criticized the condition of the food they'd been served.

Or ... I don't know exactly. Maybe something dark and spooky.

But this place just looked like a regular human bar.

There was the bar itself, a plain, reddish wood that had been varnished within an inch of its life. An array of unlabeled bottles on the wall behind it.

No mirror on that wall. But that was probably a concession to the clientele, some of whom wouldn't be able to see themselves in a mirror.

A series of small, round tables, each with four wooden chairs. A small stage off to one side, matte black.

And the windowless, wood-paneled walls, they were covered in newspaper reports. Disappearances, unexplained deaths, even stories about spontaneous human combustion.

Matte black floor. Not as sticky as a normal bar. Maybe fewer drinks were spilled here.

Or maybe that was because the place looked empty.

A dozen round tables, but no one sitting at them.

I don't mean no humans. I mean no occupants visible to my naked eye.

No customers I could see at the bar, either.

In fact, it looked for a moment as though the three of us, plus the dead doorman were the only people in the place.

"I can't believe you weren't going to let us in," I remarked, addressing the doorman for the first time, and a little proud of myself that I could do so without even a slight urge to vomit. "You guys need the custom."

"Gee," the dead guy said, glaring at me. "Wonder why everyone split when I had to let you in?"

"Not everyone," a smooth voice said.

I looked over into a doorway I hadn't seen, down just past the bar. A man stood there now. Tallish, but not as tall as me. Slender, but stylishly so. Much like the cut of his black suit. Which I thought was a bit much over a black shirt, but the moment I thought that, I realized the shirt was navy blue. It was the tie he wore that was black.

His short, styled hair was black too, as were his eyes. Only thing white about this guy was his chalk-white skin.

And the smile he gave me, it might as well have been black. It wasn't menacing. It was ... inviting. Which, in a place like this, set off little alarm bells all up and down my spine.

He walked closer.

"We're not looking for you," Des said to him, interposing himself between me and Mr. Black Suit.

"Perhaps," he said with a small smile. "But you've found me all the same, which might be to the benefit of at least one of you."

"Nope," Des said. "Turn tail and split, like your hooves."

Mr. Black Suit looked down at his shiny black shoes. Blinked innocence at Des.

"Please," Des said. "Expect *me* of all people to fall for appearances?"

"Don't be droll," Mr. Black Suit said. "It doesn't suit you." He looked past Des to me. "Now you, Selwyn, *you* look like a man of intelligence and refined tastes. Perhaps you would be so kind as to speak with me for a few moments, about what I can do for you and what you can do for me."

"Des already said it," I said, putting together the hints about tails and cloven hooves and calculating the total as *demon*. "Turn tail and split. You're not wanted here."

"He is as long as he's buying," a new voice said. And a man stood up behind the bar, holding a case of some kind of bottles.

Well, he looked like a man, at least. But in this place, I was suspecting there were only three humans.

Strike that. I wasn't sure about Des.

So two, *maybe* three humans.

But the bartender, he looked Greek. Had that kind of face, and the curly black hair, to go with the right kind of skin tone. He also had the weathered skin of a sailor. Right kind of ropy muscles for it too. In fact, even the yellow shirt he wore looked like the kind of multi-pocketed thing that would serve well on a ship of some sort.

The bartender set the case of bottles down on the bar, glared at Des, and said, "For that matter, I haven't heard any orders from you three yet, even though you bullied my doorman into letting you in."

"Please," Mr. Black Suit said. "Charge their drinks to me." He smiled at me, and it looked like the devil's smile all right. Full of teeth and a subtle kind of menace lurking just behind them.

"We pay for our own," Des said, shaking his head. "We don't need favors from the likes of you."

"I must say," Edmund said. "The reputation of your folk is that you give nothing away for free. Rather, indeed, that what appears to be freely given often comes with a higher price tag than one might imagine."

"Why are we still talking to him?" I asked.

"Who else is there to talk to?" Mr. Black Suit asked.

"Me, maybe," a voice said behind me.

A voice I recognized.

It still sounded rusty, like it didn't get used enough. High, though. And the sound of it crinkled gooseflesh all over my skin and sent creeps right up my neck.

I whirled around. My hand went to the right pocket in my cargo shorts, but Des grabbed my arm.

Still. Des didn't stop me from seeing what I needed to see.

The vampire was here.

15

———————

He hadn't changed a bit. Not a line or wrinkle, not that I'd expected him to.

It to. This was an it, not a him. I needed to keep that straight in my head.

Still five-foot-nothing. Maybe weighed a buck and a half. If that. Even with the pot belly. The ancient, torn jeans. The flannel shirt, worn open without a tee-shirt under it. Greasy, unwashed black hair.

And it still had that sneering smile.

I tried again for my stake, but Des clamped his hand on my elbow hard enough to hurt.

"Wait," Des whispered. "Striking first here is a bad idea."

That made me blink. This was the kind of detail I would like to have known in advance.

The whole point of coming to this place was that it would cut down on escape routes for the vampire. Cut down on angles of approach too. Maybe even give us some allies, since clearly it wasn't well loved in this town.

But the allies part hadn't worked. Mr. Black Suit was only going to help us if I offered my soul or something, and Todd, Page, and especially Tangi would have killed me just for considering that an option.

And the bartender, he seemed to only care about who was buying drinks in his bar.

He cared who was a *paying customer*...

"Three whiskeys," I said. "Your best scotch. Neat. Touch of water."

"Don't get much call for whisky here. I'll see what I can get you."

"Well played," Edmund breathed.

Meanwhile, the vampire stared at us, and we stared right back.

"You could have an ally in me, you know," Mr. Black Suit said. "That one, he has nothing I would want. You though, Selwyn. You certainly do."

"Not selling my soul to kill a vampire," I said, not taking my eyes off my target, which grinned even broader at my words. "Kind of defeats the point."

"You have more to offer than a soul," Mr. Black Suit said. "Come, let us discuss what you have and what you want..."

"Fuck off already," Des said.

The bartender slammed a bottle down on the bar behind me. I didn't even look. Just nodded. I could hear him pour.

"Ten," the bartender said, which told me this wouldn't be good whiskey.

Still, I tossed a twenty over my shoulder. "Keep the change."

"Well," the vampire said, taking a few steps into the bar, without actually coming any closer. "Thought I'd have to hunt you down."

That voice was painfully rough. Like every word was getting ripped out of its throat.

"You going to let your customers get harassed?" I asked the bartender, my eyes still on the vaguely approaching vampire.

"Human's got a point," the bartender said. "You drinking or fighting?"

"Both, I think," the vampire said, and that voice made me wince. Not in sympathy. Just... I don't know.

"Order something and you're a customer," the bartender said. "Don't and you're a problem."

"Fine." The vampire glanced behind us, considering the unlabeled bottles.

"You know," I whispered toward Mr. Black Suit, "I might be willing to talk with you, if I live through this. After all, once the vampire's dead and I know I'm going to live, I might want to live in style."

"Typical American," Mr. Black Suit said, disappointment in his voice. "Wanting something for nothing more than a vague promise you have no intention of fulfilling."

He disappeared in a cloud of brimstone.

I might have cricked my neck further, just whipping my head around to gawk at where he'd been, if I were willing to take my eyes off the vampire.

I wasn't though. Not even for something as surprising as a person — demon, whatever — disappearing in a cloud of brimstone.

"No," the vampire said. "You have nothing I want. Not in bottles."

"Order or leave," the bartender said. And there was something different about his voice. Not menacing, just ... confident. As though, whatever the bartender was, he was certain in his ability to hold his own against a vampire.

Which made me all the gladder that right now he was on my side.

"In fact," the bartender added, "you better have a damned good order. It's your fault these three are here, and your fault most of my customers won't be coming in tonight."

The vampire went through the motions of sighing deeply, without a hint of audible breath.

He reached into his pocket. Pulled out a decrepit velvet pouch. Tossed it through the air toward the bartender.

The bartender whistled. "This real?"

"It is," Des said.

He hadn't looked over. Far as I could tell, he had no way of knowing what was in that pouch. All the same, he said those words with his usual complete confidence. If anything, he made his words sound a little sour, as though disappointed in having to admit to a truth he didn't like.

"Bon appetite," the bartender said.

The vampire turned to face the three of us.

Between me and that vampire, only one table and its four little chairs.

The vampire picked that table up and threw it against the wall.

THE TABLE EXPLODED AGAINST THE WOOD PANELS OF THE WALL.

Des leapt into the air.

But the vampire was already on the move.

Edmund had whipped out two things, even before I could get my stake out: a vial of what had to be holy water in one hand, and a bible in the other.

Neither helped him.

The vampire ripped his head right off.

The tearing sound was a hideous thing to hear. Fast as it was, it was a sound that went straight to my guts. Tried to turn them to water. It was a sound I can hear to this day. Wake up sometimes, screaming when the sound comes into my dreams.

Blood fountained up out of Edmund's neck with more pressure than I would have believed possible for such a frail-looking body.

Des slipped up behind the vampire. Ready to grab it while it fed.

The vampire took no more than a sip of Edmund's blood before whirling to face Des.

They grappled each other. Des grabbed the vampire's shoulders. The vampire grabbed Des' neck.

I had the stake out now.

And the vampire' nose came up like it smelled the holly.

The vampire flung Des at a wall. Spun to leap over the nearest table toward the exit.

And I did what I did best.

I tacked that dead thing like a running back who thought he had a clear path to the end zone.

The vampire might have been as strong as a semi, but it only weighed maybe two-fifths what I did. Plus I had momentum on my side, and training (if a little rust in my technique).

I plowed into it and slammed the two of us into the floor.

My stake flew out of my hand. Bounced along the floor toward the bar.

The vampire grinned up at me like I'd just played into its trap.

It grabbed me by the shoulders. Pulled me closer.

I put both hands on the floor. Fought with every ounce of strength in my body. Fought to keep my neck from its fangs.

And I could see those fangs now. Long and sharp and whiter than the rest of the fiend's yellowed teeth.

Its breath reached me too. Rancid road kill didn't smell as bad as this thing's breath. Made me throw up on the fiend, but that only widened its grin.

Des was there then. Grabbed one of the creature's wrists, muttering in that weird language of his. Tried to free me.

But the vampire kept inching me closer to those fangs.

My life began to flash before my eyes. I shook my head to clear it. I needed to stay here and now. I needed to not give in.

Giving in. Surrendering to those fangs. That would be so easy. So easy with that inevitable strength pulling me ever closer.

I could feel death calling for me. Offering me reunion with my friends.

Des let go of the wrist. Stood. Pulled back to kick.

The vampire leapt to its feet, still holding me.

My hands were on nothing now.

Des was gone. The vampire had done something. Kicked him maybe. I was vaguely aware that I could hear something heavy crash.

My neck, exposed to the vampire's fangs now.

My hands, flailing in the air behind the vampire. No way to keep myself free and alive.

Burning pain as those fangs entered my throat. Tearing my flesh.

My pounding heart only sped the flow of my blood out through that hole. Into the sucking-gobbling mouth of the fiend.

All these years, for nothing.

All this effort, for nothing.

I was about to die.

But then, something was thrust into my hand.

Something round. Solid. Wooden.

The stake!

Des had to have gotten me the stake.

I didn't waste any time. The world was already starting to fade around me. Tunneling down to black. My pounding heart slowing. Fluttering.

And the creature sucked harder and harder on the wound.

No idea what strength I had left. Felt as though I couldn't even break skin right now, much less ribs and a heart.

But I had the stake. I had to try.

I screamed defiance at the vampire as I swung that stake with everything I had left inside me.

I didn't aim, but I felt the stake shift my hand, even while my arm was swinging.

Edmund's spell, or whatever he'd done. Even dead, Edmund was still helping me when I needed it the most.

And Edmund's spell guided my hand. I struck true.

And either the chest of a vampire is more vulnerable than a human rib cage...

No.

That was a scientific answer. This was a creature that didn't exist in the eyes of physics.

The holly stake pierced the vampire's heart and struck it down, because that was the right weapon to kill it. Not ultraviolet lights. Not wooden pellets in a shotgun shell.

A holly stake. Delivered in a single blow, straight through the heart.

The creature screamed as it released me. I immediately grabbed my neck, applying all the pressure I could, even as I was still blacking out.

I bit the inside of my mouth. Clenched every muscle in my body. Did everything I could think of to remain conscious until I knew for certain that the vampire was dead.

If fell writhing to the bar floor. Blood pouring out of the wound.

Way more blood than its little body could hold. Gallons and gallons of blood. More blood than a jet airliner full of people could have produced.

And still it screamed and writhed. Crumpling as I watched.

And Des, he took a wicked looking combat knife and silenced the screaming by cutting off the vampire's head.

And then, all at once, it crumbled to dust.

That was when I blacked out.

I CAME TO, WHICH SURPRISED ME AS MUCH AS ANYTHING EVER HAD. I was sure I was a dead man. Deader than the doorman, who was standing over Des' shoulders, while Des crouched over me.

"Slow," Des said, one hand on my shoulder. "Don't try to get up yet. You'll be able to soon. But not yet."

"How…" I croaked, but couldn't get the rest of the question out.

Des answered it anyway.

"Death is truth, and life is truth. But you, you were in between," he said. He smiled. "You had your choice of truths, and I made you pick. You chose life. That meant that what healing I could do would bring you back."

"Ed…" I started coughing.

"Edmund," Des said through a long sigh. "It's too late for him. We'll give him a hell of a sendoff. Don't you worry in the meantime. I'm not rich as that boy was, but I can manage just fine."

I tried to ask about a dozen questions then, but not one of them could come out.

Des gave me time.

"The stake. How?" I asked, pleased that my voice was stronger already.

A rough voice cleared itself.

I looked over at the dead doorman.

"Well," he said. "My boss didn't say I *couldn't* help you. And I don't particularly care for vampires. Plus ... well ... we don't get very many good tippers in here."

I started laughing, which turned into coughing before making its way back to laughter.

When I could speak — and sit up, which was a plus — I said, "You helped me because I tipped well?"

"You tipped a hundred percent on a bar tab," the dead doorman said. "That's worth encouraging."

Des clapped me on the shoulder.

But then I saw Edmund again. His poor, headless body lying on the barroom floor. Des said Edmund was beyond *his* healing...

I looked over at the doorman. "I don't suppose you know anyone who could—"

"Just the guy you said you didn't want to talk to."

"No," Des said. "Edmund wouldn't want to come back that way." Des helped me to my feet. Dusted me off, and added. "Besides, he didn't really expect to survive this. He wasn't exactly a young man."

"Neither are you."

"Yes, but for me, time is a distraction, not a truth."

"What?" I said.

Des grinned at me. "Sure you want to know?"

"No," I said, shaking my head. "I'm pretty sure I don't."

WE GOT EDMUND'S BODY BACK TO THE HOTEL IN A COFFIN — apparently this was the kind of bar that kept spare coffins in the back — but Des assured the hotel management that it was a prop, and they believed him.

Des and I agreed that we wanted the local authorities to know as little as possible about what had happened here tonight.

The bartender — whose name I never did catch, and I think I'm grateful — thanked us for that. Apparently he wasn't any more eager for legal attention than we were.

We stayed at the Usher for two more days while I finished recuperating. Frankly, I couldn't believe how fast I was healing. But when I asked Des about it, he gave me an answer that was longwinded, dealt a good deal with truth and distraction, and in the end told me next to nothing.

The answer, far as I was concerned, was "magic." And at this point, it was an answer I could accept.

Next to nothing was about as much as I understood of Des' explanation of why he hadn't been more help in the fight against the vampire. He'd intimated several times that he'd fought and killed multiple vampires, but the one I fought beside him threw Des around like a ragdoll.

Des did have an answer for that. Something involving types of vampires and changing vulnerabilities and the spells he tried that should have worked, but didn't.

I'd asked him why truth didn't help there.

"They're innately creatures of distraction," he'd said, "but the nature of the distraction varies from breed to breed. Finding the right truth to unweave that one would have taken time I couldn't afford."

Again, not a very satisfying answer. Not unless I wanted to learn a whole lot more about things I wasn't sure I wanted to know in the first place.

I knew now that vampires were real. And ghouls, and demons, psychics and magic. Hadn't seen any ghosts, so far as I could be certain, but those were probably real too.

Didn't have any evidence I could have shown the Pages and Todds of the world, but I wasn't in a hurry to do that anyway.

After all, the last time I'd tried telling anyone the truth about vampires, it had cost me eight years of my life and they'd managed to convince me I was wrong.

I had no interest in going through any of that again.

No, this was a truth I'd keep to myself. Maybe write down in my later years, and leave to be discovered after my death. I'd dedicate that memoir to Page, Tangi and Todd. A last promise to their memory, before I finally let myself say goodbye.

Once I was healed enough to leave the Usher, there was the matter of Edmund's death and funeral to deal with.

Turned out that Edmund's primary residence was in Virginia. Des and I held the service there, after Des had gotten a friendly coroner to log Edmund's death as a hunting accident.

Leave it to Des to make a truth sound like a lie.

When it came to the funeral, we needed a bigger venue than we'd expected. We'd made arrangements with Saint Peter's, in Norfolk, which was a pretty darn big cathedral.

But Edmund had touched many, many lives. And it seemed that every one of those lives wanted to come pay his or her respects to the passing of Edmund Xerxes.

Might have helped that the newspaper didn't run his obituary in the little spot we'd paid for, but instead ran a full, front-page story about the man's life and his charity work, and mentioned twice the date, time and location of the service.

Speaking of charity work, all of his considerable estate was split among about a dozen charities. Even in death, the man was giving.

The day after the funeral, Des put me on a plane with a first class ticket. Gave me an odd, six-digit phone number and told me to call him if I ever needed help.

The flight back was uneventful. But when I got home, waiting on my doorstep for me was a package, delivered by courier. Inside, a handwritten book, with a note attached.

My dear Selwyn,

It is my firm belief that there is no point in publishing this, my treatise on the development and application of extranormal skills, as those who truly seek such skills will find methods anyway, and those who do not will not benefit from reading what I have written.

Nevertheless, I leave the decision to you. Publish this if you like. Read it and develop skills of your own, if you wish. Or merely read it, and perhaps understand me a little better.

It has been an honor to know you.

Sincerely yours,

Edmund Xerxes

I sat there on the hot bricks of my porch and whistled. This was hundreds of pages, complete with diagrams and what looked to be pretty thorough instructions.

"Damn it, Edmund," I whispered to the skies. "I just wanted to get back to my life."

Maybe, if I was lucky, even forget that the things that went bump in the night were real. Pretend to the blissful ignorance of most of humanity.

But the book in my hands now, it felt heavy with responsibility.

I could still see the faces of those hundreds, maybe thousands of people who had come to Edmund's funeral. The people who had been helped by Edmund. All lives he'd changed for the better.

And that didn't even include me, the man he'd died helping.

Edmund was dead because he'd helped me. That was a truth I didn't need Des to show me.

I owed it to Edmund's memory to pick up his torch. Develop some "extranormal skills" of my own, and help others the way Edmund had. Page, Tangi and Todd would have approved, I think.

But in the meantime, I had phone calls to make. There were Hollywood companies hot to hire me for my sound work, and maybe it was time I took them up on that. Got a real job. Maybe even met a girl.

The Vultures, they didn't seem as scary to me anymore.

After all, I knew there were real terrors in the darkness.

And what was more, I knew they could be beaten.

SIGN UP FOR STEFON'S NEWSLETTER

Stefon loves to keep in touch with his readers, and loves to keep you reading. The best way for him to do both is for you to sign up for his newsletter.

Sign up at http://www.stefonmears.com/join

If you sign up for Stefon's newsletter, you get...

- Monthly updates about his publishing and travel schedules
- His latest news, in brief, and answers to reader questions
- A free short story for signing up
- List-only offers and occasional specials
- Plus a free short story every month!

ABOUT THE AUTHOR

Stefon Mears has personally identified more than two dozen types of vampires. Stefon has more than thirty books to his credit, and he never stops writing. He earned his M.F.A. in Creative Writing from N.I.L.A., and his B.A. in Religious Studies (double emphasis in Ritual and Mythology) from U.C. Berkeley. He's a lifelong gamer and fantasy fan. Stefon lives in Portland, Oregon, with his wife and three cats.

Look for Stefon online:
www.stefonmears.com
himself@stefonmears.com